And So It
Begins

Hayward Dennis

AND SO IT BEGINS

This is a work of fiction. All of the characters, names, incidents, organizations, and dialogue in this novel are either the products of the author's imagination or are used fictitiously.

iUniverse books may be ordered through booksellers or by contacting:

iUniverse
1663 Liberty Drive
Bloomington, IN 47403
www.iuniverse.com
1-800-Authors (1-800-288-4677)

ISBN: 978-1-5320-7924-5 (sc)
ISBN: 978-1-5320-7926-9 (hc)
ISBN: 978-1-5320-7925-2 (e)

Library of Congress Control Number: 2019911319

Print information available on the last page.

iUniverse rev. date: 08/09/2019

Contents

If Father is from everlasting to everlasting,
then where are we in eternity?

CHAPTER 1

D

He had another sleepless night. For several nights D's dreams had been full of troubling images, images that seemed so very real. They were like coded messages that sparked a burning flame deep in his soul. They were like some premonition of something or some event that would soon come. The dreams made him shiver with both fear and anticipation. The problem was that D had no idea of what the dreams meant. He could handle nightmares, but this was totally a different beast.

He struggled out of bed, still dazed by what he had seen in his dream. He tried to maintain his usual morning ritual of first, making up his bed, taking a piss, shaving, washing his face, and finally, putting on fresh cloths. This morning, however, felt awkward and strange. The dream's images continued to flash in his mind's eye. To say the least, he was deeply troubled. Still, he had to get to work, dream or not.

D managed to complete his morning habit and walked to the kitchen for breakfast. Living alone had its perks, for he didn't have to be subject to anyone but himself. He thought about a big breakfast but decided on a bowl of cereal. When he sat down to eat, an image from the dream flashed in his bowl of cereal. *Man, am I going crazy*, he thought. *I'd better talk to one of my friends about this.*

When D finished breakfast, he looked at his watch. He made a habit of going to work thirty minutes early. He was just made that way. He gathered his wallet, car keys, and jacket and started for the front door. He just couldn't shake the eerie feeling he felt from the dream. Still, he had to get to work, but he hoped that his day would get better. As he began to lock up, he realized that he'd forgotten his cell phone. He walked back into the house to get it. Suddenly, he abruptly stopped as he peered into what looked like one of the images from his dream. "What the ..." he said and winced.

The image was that of pure light shaped in the figure of a person. D could not recognize or even see a face, just a bright figure. He shook his head, wondering what it could be, whatever it was. He wanted to speak. No, he desperately tried to speak, but no words would come. Not only that, but he felt paralyzed, unable to move or to even breathe. *Is this what being terrified feels like?* He thought. He could feel his hands becoming sweaty and cold. His legs trembled like that of a winter's chill. Yeah, he was terrified!

The image just stood there, bright but beguiling. D had heard about demons and spirits and ghosts, but which was this ... this thing? Fear began to grip his thoughts. He had to stay calm. He remembered the Sunday school lessons he'd been taught as a child, so he began to quote whatever scriptures came to mind. At that moment the bright figure moved slightly but noticeably. D stopped thinking as he heard another voice speaking to him, but this one was in his head! It was a soothing, comforting, and persuasive voice. D stopped feeling afraid. His legs stopped trembling. Even his hands felt flushed with warm blood again. The voice in his head just didn't speak to his mind, but it spoke like a commanding horn piercing his soul.

"Wh... is it that you want from me?" D asked, stuttering. The figure stepped closer toward him. D could hear clearly the voice speaking in his mind. Was this how telepathy worked? Memories rushed through his mind, causing D to temporarily lose the figure's voice in his head. He had to calm down, take control of himself, and not be afraid. The figure's voice paused as if he knew about the struggle D was having in staying calm. The situation was bizarre, to say the least. D had never felt so out of it. He had to shake off the gripping fear that was trying to overtake him. He tried to close his eyes, hoping that he could wish the figure away. Still, the figure's voice spoke to his mind, calmingly, peacefully.

"I am not here to bring you harm," the figure said. "I have been sent to equip you for the coming war ahead."

D could only stand there. It felt as if some force had taken over and frozen him. *War? What war?* D thought. He managed to utter a question out loud to the figure. "What war are you talking about?" he asked. D waited for the answer that seemed to take an eternity. The figure stepped closer. D could sense that the figure was not hostile. Even so, he had to stay on his guard.

"The war that was prophesied at the beginning of the creation," the figure said.

"You mean, Armageddon?" D awkwardly asked again out loud.

"No," the figure responded.

D was freaking out by now. Here he was having a Q and A with a ghost or something—telepathically! He wanted to shout and call out for help, but his mouth was silent while his mind screamed. He mustered up the courage to calm himself and ask the figure another question. "If it's not Armageddon, then what war?"

The figure seemed to look at D as though slicing deep into his very being. When the figure spoke again, it was like a light was illuminated inside of D, a light of complete understanding. "Humankind was created in the likeness of the Creator. You and the rest of humanity are body, soul, and spirit. Think of yourself as a spirit in a vessel or a spirit in a bottle where the bottle is your container or the outer shell, which is your body. The real you, that which is eternal and the most precious part of you, is your spirit. I am here to give you the gifts that you will need from the Creator so that you can help in the victory that must come to pass."

D was flabbergasted! What he was hearing confused him and greatly overwhelmed all that he had previously believed. He'd read and had been taught about the end times, but if this war was not about Armageddon but something different— Man, this was freaky! He took a long, drawn-out, deep breath before he then dared to ask another question. "B ... but why me?"

Before the figure answered, he made a sweeping gesture with what appeared to be a hand. The entire room vanished, and they were in what looked like another world. D could only marvel at what he saw. The scene before him was like nothing he'd ever seen before, not in books or even movies. What he was looking at could be described only as ...

a creepy moment! The light was so clear that it stunned the eyes, but it did not hurt or blind. The air was extremely fresh, though he was not breathing through his nose. Rather he was breathing through his whole being! There were trees and patches of green grass so full of color that no painting could depict them. Even the blue permeating the sky was simply awesome! Where were they? What part of Earth ... or the universe were they in? Had the figure led him to another dimension?

"Where are we?" D asked, mumbling.

"We are standing at the time of creation," the figure answered.

"If this is the moment of creation, then where are the animals and humans?" D asked.

"The Creator has not created them yet," answered the figure. "This is what the Creator wanted me to show you before I begin giving you the gifts that you will need."

Talk about tripping! D had no idea about what was happening. His mind only reeled over what he was seeing and hearing. "Again, why me?" D quietly asked.

"A promise was made to your ancestors by the Creator, and He keeps His promises," said the figure.

Curious, D asked, "What promise?"

The figure gestured again with his hand, closed the wonder before them, and opened up another scene. D saw what looked like the picture of an African village. He saw some very dark-skinned people moving about. Some were cooking, while others were washing what looked like clothing. He could see children running about as though playing some game. He noticed a group of mothers sitting, suckling their babies as they talked in a language unknown to him. *Where is this place?* He thought. The figure obviously had heard him think and quickly answered, "We are in an African village, a tribe that existed many millennia ago and whose generations are in you. It was with them that the Creator made the promise."

D could only listen in awe. He'd heard about such talk where ancestors looked down from heaven and helped us, but he never put much credence behind it. Yet this figure, who must have been an angel, was teaching him about a truth he'd denied. D could only shake his head with doubt. The figure must have sensed D's inner turmoil as it spoke again, "You must not be afraid. The Creator made this promise to your ancestors because of their love and devotion to Him, and He always keeps His promises."

Before D could catch himself, he blurted out, "Okay, exactly what promise did God make to them?"

"The promise that the first would be last and the last first," the figure said.

"The first shall be last … and the last shall be first," D mumbled. He was even more lost in understanding, for he'd always thought that such riddles were just scriptural nonsense and that no one really fully understood or was ever meant to understand. D could feel that the figure sensed his confusion, so the figure spoke again, only this time with more clarity.

"The Word of God is a coded book just like a cipher that must be decoded. Many have tried to understand its message but have fallen short. Only those whom God has anointed are able to decode or understand the written Word." The figure paused, waiting for D's reaction. D stood rigid and bewildered but with intense interest. He didn't want to appear stupid, but what else could he be, especially since he had no idea what to say. After a time of silence, the figure continued, "I am the decoder. Many know me as the Comforter, the Holy Ghost, or the Spirit of God."

Like a bolt of lightning, D was shocked into realization! Of course, he should have known that the figure before him was indeed a heavenly body, but he never guessed that it was the Spirit of God Himself! His excitement must have been obvious, for D could sense the Spirit of God smiling at him. "Now that you know who I am, your training can begin," He said. "You must not be afraid of what you hear or see, for I will guide you through the journey. Remember I am the Comforter, the revealer of God's Word. What I am about to teach you only a few have been privileged to know. God is not man but much, much more. He lives in a plain of existence that supersedes all understanding. His Word is alive and vibrant, able to create." The Spirit paused at this point to allow what He'd said to sink into D's thoughts. Then He continued,

"You have been called to do His will at a time that was preordained from the beginning. He has instilled in you all that you will need to accomplish His will. Again, I say, be not afraid, for I am with you forever."

When the Spirit said that, D's knees wanted to buckle, but a force steadied him. He began to realize that it was the power of God around him that strengthened him. He felt calm and quite at peace. He'd remembered his days in Sunday school and the many times in church when the people would sing gospel songs and praised the Lord. He remembered that one time when he became so enthralled in the praises of God that he felt like he was lighter than air. It was this same feeling that he now was feeling. Tears began to run down his cheeks, not tears of hurt or pain but of joy—insatiable joy! He could sense the face of the Spirit smiling as if He was deeply approving of what was happening. And before D could relax himself, he began to shout in a language he'd never heard before, a language filled with power and glory! D had no idea about what he was saying, but he could feel his inner self leave his body. What was happening?! He felt both afraid and excited! He felt himself going higher and higher from where he had stood! "My God!" he heard his mind scream, while his voice continued speaking in that unknown language.

D did not know just how long he stayed in that state of mind, but when he came back to himself, he saw the Spirit standing watch. "I am with you ... always, even to the end of the world," He said, comforting D.

D had many questions to ask, but the Spirit spoke again before he could speak. "The language you just now spoke was that of your ancestors, a tongue long since forgotten. The enemy forced it from your ancestors because the enemy feared its power. Your ancestors were chosen by God, and so they became the focus of the enemy's rage and hate." The Spirit paused so that D could gather himself, for the Spirit did not want to educate D too fast. After all, what D had to learn was so very important for the mission that lay ahead.

"In the beginning God created the heaven and the earth," the Spirit slowly continued. "Many without the decoder thought that it was the time of Adam and Eve, but there was a world before that time, a most glorious world when the angels praised and sang melodically to God. But it was not to last. A usurper, one who wanted to exalt himself above God, deceived many of the heavenly host, and so plotted to overtake God's throne. There was war, and the faithful to God cast the deceiver and his followers down to earth, where the cities of earth were destroyed. The earth became dark, and the waters covered it all."

D trembled. He was talking about the book of Genesis! "I always thought there was only one planet with life upon it," D interrupted.

"Many have also, but now you know the truth. The deceiver was once a very prominent angel of God. He commanded the day. He was the sun of the morning. Without him, the earth had no light. When he fell, that is—when he rebelled against God—the light of God was withdrawn from him, and all that was left was darkness. And so earth became covered with darkness."

D sighed. He almost had tears in his eyes. He felt the Word of truth surging through his being. Doubt and mistrust faded away. He began to embrace the truth. His heart felt free, and his mind lighter. He had always wondered why the book of Genesis stated dark sighing waters at the beginning and why God had created such. The truth was there all along, only he did not have the decoder to see it. Now he began to see more clearly. Before D could speak again, the Holy Spirit spoke.

"You have been called, even before you entered into your mother's womb. Your calling is one of great importance that will shape the days ahead. But first, you must be anointed with gifts to allow you to accomplish the will of God."

"Anointed?" D asked, almost stammering the word out.

"Yes," responded the Holy Spirit. "Those whom God calls He qualifies. He anoints them with His gifts to accomplish their mission. Be not afraid, for I will always be with you to guide you through whatever darkness that may come."

The Holy Spirit then came closer to D. Only pure light was radiating before D's eyes. He still could not see a face, only the outline of a figure. As the Holy Spirit came even closer, a peace that was never known to D engulfed his entire being. He felt no fear of anything at all! His fear about dogs from an unfortunate experience as a boy vanished. He just stood still and allowed the Holy Spirit to come closer. Suddenly, D could sense that he was no longer standing but somehow immersed in the very essence of the Holy Spirit! He wanted to cry, not for fear or dismay but for joy. The joy he felt was like nothing he'd felt in his life! It was as though only that which was good and perfect existed! Was he in some kind of bubble, or was he still in his house? Either way, he didn't care. He only began to delight in what was happening.

D could sense himself, and yet he could sense the Spirit. It was as though they had become one mind but still remained two. He tried not to overthink what was happening, especially as his tears became more apparent. Without thinking, words began to flow from his mouth, words that he did not recognize. They sounded like some foreign language! The strange thing was that he could understand the words, but he still managed to keep control of his thoughts. *What's going on?* he heard himself think.

D did not notice how much time passed while he was in … whatever trance he was experiencing. Only when he had stopped speaking and weeping did he fear that time had passed. He looked at his watch then. No time had elapsed! Surely, he had been there for more than an hour! Then a weird thought crossed his mind. Had he been abducted by aliens? Was the whole conversation with the Holy Spirit a dream? He looked at his hands and then around the room. He shook himself to make sure that he was himself.

The experience made him a bit unnerved. He wanted to believe that he'd had an encounter with God, but he did not want to entertain doubt, no matter what. He could sense that doubt was not supposed to have any place in his thoughts. What then should he believe? As though by instinct, he fell on his knees and faced the floor. He began to call upon the name of the Lord for help. He needed confirmation about what had happened. Was what he had just experienced truly from God? He had not prayed like this for years, remembering his time years ago in the church. He could feel that his prayer was reaching Heaven as he eased up his head, expecting to see the Holy Spirit. He didn't. What he did sense was an inner voice within him, one assuring him and comforting him. The Spirit was now a part of D. No longer was the Holy Spirit some eerie bright light, but He lived in him! His thoughts were like communicating with the Spirit of God! "Okay," he said. "What is it that you want of me now?"

D did not expect the reply he got. The Spirit spoke plainly to his heart and said that D had been anointed with the gift of tongues. D listened intently, for he really wanted to know. The Spirit continued telling D that he would need not only the gift of tongues to communicate with those he encountered but the gift of healing, which he now also had been given. D stood as if paralyzed, not so much with fear but in awe. He remembered his Bible study classes from back in the day and how such spiritual gifts were sometimes given to believers. *But why me?* he thought. D had not been the most devout of believers. In fact, he thought of himself as a lost soul. Immediately, the Spirit rebuked D's thoughts and told him that it was never about what things he'd done but rather the promise made to his ancestors by God.

Sometimes it was best to simply accept what happened to you. This was the case with D. He felt like a new person, no longer bound by the fears of his past or the guilt of wrongdoings. It was like he'd been soaked with fresh water from head to toe! He felt cleansed!

As D became more relaxed, he awkwardly began to walk about, trying to gather himself so that he could go to work. Though his thoughts were there, the Spirit had another. The Spirit wanted D to stand still, for there was yet another gift D had to receive, the word of knowledge. D admitted that he never understood such a gift. Though he had heard ministers preach about it and even had read some articles on it, he still did not understand the gift. Still, he stopped his preparation for work and listened to what the Spirit had to say.

Since the Spirit was no longer in the form of a brilliant figure, D found it both strange and comforting as he listened to the Spirit speak to him. It was as though D now had two distinct minds sharing one mind. He knew that if he was to learn how God was going to use him, he needed to know all that the Spirit had to teach him. And so he stood still to listen most intently.

The Spirit began, "The gift that is the Word of knowledge is quite simple to understand. It is the knowledge that you'll need at the time to help in a situation—and that means in any situation."

D was stunned. He'd never heard it put so simply before. "I told you that I was the decoder of God's Word," the Spirit assured D, knowing his thoughts. "The Word of God is alive, and knowledge is a part of that life-giving power. You will need God's knowledge if you are to accomplish what must be done, for the battles you will face are treacherous indeed. Many will need your help to survive. You must know when to use the gift of healing and you must know what knowledge to impart to those in a circumstance." D's mouth widened in disbelief. The Spirit continued, "Not all will be of God's promise … not all are bloodstained."

"Okay," D said out loud. "What does that mean?"

Before he could ask another question, D heard the Spirit explain, "The precious blood of the Lamb of God has been given to all who will accept. It is this blood that tells you who are of God's flock and who will adhere to His Word. It is these anointed ones whom you will help in the war to come."

"How?" D asked. "How will I know who they are? Will I see blood upon them, and if so, where?" The Spirit knew D's frustration, so the Spirit comforted him. "D, I will give you the gift of discernment of the spirits. You will know those who belong to God and those who are of the adversary, the chief of the fallen angels whom you call the devil."

D trembled at these words. He'd heard stories about this bogeyman all his life, but he had never taken them seriously. Fear tried to grip him, but the Spirit steadied him. He could feel the power of God surging through his being. "I'm sorry," D said to the Holy Spirit.

"You don't need to apologize," the Holy Spirit said. "The war you will face is lined with such perils and moments of fear. But remember that I am with you … always."

Such words reassured D. He needed them. He began to tear up, not because he felt ashamed of his ignorance but because he felt so much joy. He knew that if he was to succeed, he had to be genuine and honest, not just with God but also with himself. He was flawed, and here the

Spirit of God was teaching him how to conduct spiritual warfare! "Oh, how great art thou, O Lord!" D shouted.

The Holy Spirit continued D's training. "You will know the enemy from those whom the Lord has called. The power of discernment is like a beacon shinning upon the chosen of God. Not only will you know them, but you will know how to minister unto them. If they are hurt or in need of healing, you will do whatever is needed."

D could only cringe at such responsibility. He began to feel overwhelmed at such a thought. But then he felt the tugging from the Holy Spirit, reassuring him that he was not alone. D didn't want to be like some bigheaded power monger, but he didn't want to appear too shy about what he was chosen to do either. He could sense the Holy Spirit monitoring his inner struggle, and he could sense the Spirit's wave of love and understanding. D couldn't help but fall to his knees in a fit of rushing tears. He began to praise God with words of devout adoration and love. He cried aloud, hoping that no neighbor would hear, and at the same time, he didn't care!

The Holy Spirit waited patiently for D to finish his moment of worship before He spoke to D again. "This is why you have been called. You are humble and a worshipper of God. The more you walk with Him, the more confident you will become in what you must do. Remember I and God are one, as He is one with His Word."

D stood up. He wiped the tears from his eyes. He took the handkerchief that he kept in his back pocket and blew his nose. He felt like a little child on his first day of kindergarten. He knew that the Spirit did not mind his behavior. Still, D had to allow the Holy Spirit to complete the training.

The Spirit comforted D, not by speaking but by a gentle nudge. He was trying to encourage D that the battle was not D's but the Lord's. "Now you will know them by the stain of blood. You will see them through the eyes of your spirit, for we are now one. Be encouraged, for you will do well. With the gift of tongues, you will be able to speak to them. With the gift of healing, you will be able to make them well. With the gift of knowledge, you will understand how to help them, and with the gift of discernment, you will know those who are with the enemy."

D sat down. He had to. His whole being felt like it was on fire. His head was in a daze—not a crazy daze but a good one. His excitement was without words. He felt like he had been in the presence of God Himself! He felt so light. Thoughts began to flood his mind, and he knew right away they were not his, for he'd never thought of such wonders before. He now knew that whenever he or anyone sincerely rendered praise to God, His Spirit was abiding there. It was like you had entered into God's Holy of Holies! Wow! Also, when you prayed with faith in the name of God's Son, Jesus, you were no longer just on earth, but your spirit was in the very presence of God the Father!

D's thoughts nearly blew him away. He then thought about work. He had to leave, or he'd be late. But when he looked at his watch again, he saw that no time had passed! What was going on? Surely, he had spent hours in that room. Then he heard the voice of the Spirit speak to him. His voice was calming and very assuring.

"Time is outside of the realm of God. Whenever a believer is in the presence of God and is receiving counsel, time is not measured as you normally think. You see, D, humans are body, soul, and spirit, and it is the spiritual part that was created into God's image, not the flesh. Remember what I taught you earlier, specifically that your body is but a shell, a bottle, a vessel. The real you is spirit. Your soul is the emotional and intellect that is connected to the spirit. This is the reason that when you dream, you wonder why your dreams seem to be in riddles."

D sighed, but he did not want to seem vague or to appear overwhelmed. He knew that the Spirit was teaching him, and so he had to be patient. He began to walk aimlessly about until the Spirit spoke again. "D, I know you are trying to understand a great deal. Relax. I am imparting all that you need to know and understand. You only need but to trust Me, for I will be with you always. I will never let you fail. Just trust Me."

D felt more relaxed. He shrugged away the many negative thoughts trying to flood his mind. He realized that he had to abandon everything that he thought he knew about spiritual matters, including what preachers had tried to teach him. He was being taught by the master Himself! He felt highly privileged!

"D, you must want what I must teach you. I will do so in a spirit walk."

"A what?" D asked.

"I must teach you in the spirit what you must know. Be not afraid, a spirit walk is easy, and it's an effective tool. It is almost like being in a dream, only it is for a lifetime. Remember God is outside of your realm of time and space."

D was both excited and a bit apprehensive. He remembered some whopper dreams—dreams that had him shaking once awakened. Yet he trusted the Spirit to lead him. So far the Spirit had done him no harm. Still, D could not help but wonder why he had to be taught in a spirit walk. Why not continue what he was doing now? He awkwardly asked the Spirit what they would do if someone came looking for him or if the phone rang ... or— Then D stopped himself. No, he had to trust God without doubt and with all his heart. Once again, he relaxed like a baby boy in his mother's arms.

"What now?" D asked. "What is it ... I mean, do I stand here, or do I go to bed?" Almost without another thought, D was translocated. He immediately saw a brilliant light. Then he saw the bluest of skies. He felt his body being gently controlled. *It must be the Spirit*, he thought. D allowed the Spirit full control, for he realized that he was in good hands. He could smell the fresh air around him. He heard birds singing nearby. He could feel the grass beneath his feet. *Where is this place?* he asked himself. The answer was instant as he realized that he was in the same place the Spirit had shown him before. D then heard voices. He now understood the language that the voices spoke. The Spirit was right to give him the gift of tongues. His excitement was apparent as he looked around to discover the source of the voices.

The Spirit calmly spoke to D's heart. "While you are here, you will experience a lifetime among these people. Here I will teach and train you how to use your gifts so that you will be proficient in the war to come."

"Bu ... but ..." D stopped himself. He had to trust the Spirit. He remembered what the Spirit had told him about time, namely that time was outside of God. He felt at ease again. *A lifetime*, he thought. *Well, bring it on!* Being led by the Spirit, D walked toward the dark-skinned people. He noticed that he had on clothing similar to that of the people before him, including the sandals on his feet. Yeah, D was ready. His training had begun.

CHAPTER 2
Spirit Walk

When D returned from his spirit walk, he figured that he would look like some shriveled old man with gray hairs and a beard. To his surprise, not only was he not old, but when he looked at his watch, the time was still the same as it had been when he had left! He was thoroughly excited. He remembered everything, and I mean everything! The things he'd learned were simply awesome! His experiences with the people in the spirit walk were very real and quite personal. He'd learned how to use the gift of healing. He had encountered other races and had perfected the gift of tongues as he mingled among them. The Word of knowledge had helped him when he'd needed, but most of all, D fully understood why he needed the gift of discernment. He'd helped the people to avoid trap after trap and even war by recognizing enemies seeking to enslave those he had grown to love. But perhaps the one thing that D was really excited about was how the Sprit had taught him spiritual warfare.

Spiritual warfare is just like it sounds. You war in the realm of the spirit. It is nothing like the wars fought in the flesh or in the realm of the physical. D had learned that those who are called and who are true believers can approach the throne of God without fear or guilt because the only thing that Father sees is the bloodstained soul of the believer. No longer was D ashamed or fearful when he prayed. He knew now that he had complete favor with the Father. Whenever he prayed now, he went boldly before the throne, and he believed that whatever he petitioned God, he would receive. He'd learned how to battle the powers of darkness through spiritual warfare. When he entered into the battle, it was his spirit that was there, and he would use the weapons of the Holy Spirit to defeat any of the enemy's tactics. There was the time when he used spiritual warfare to ward off the plague that the enemy had set upon the villagers. He had used the gift of tongues with the unknown language that only the Father could understand. He commanded the evil spirits attacking the village to leave. It was not D who had done it, but the power of Father Himself within D.

D looked around the room, stretched, and walked to the kitchen for a glass of water. He felt so refreshed and so very light. He noticed that he was not hungry or tired. Still, the experience left him with two questions: How was the war the Spirit had talked about going to occur, and when would it arrive?

D also wondered about work. He tried to hear what the Spirit had to say about it; however, he heard nothing but silence. He had learned from his training in the spirit walk that the Spirit would speak in His own time. That left D with thoughts about the days ahead. His job was not a difficult one. He pretty much worked alone tending to shrubbery around the city. Being a city employee was not that bad, though sometimes the personalities of the bosses and workers got in the way. Knowing what he knew now caused him to shudder with some deep concern. However, he'd learned how to scatter demons in spiritual combat. Would that work here in the real world? He thought he'd find out.

CHAPTER 3
The Spirit Walk's Reality

D gathered his car keys and work items. He opened the house door, paused, and then looked back. He thought that he would see the Spirit standing in His brilliant light like before. Almost automatically, he remembered that the Spirit was abiding in him! He smiled and closed the door, locking it behind him.

As D drove down the street to his job, he could feel that something had changed. Was it the city or the world, or was it him? Whatever it was, he began to see things differently. He saw auras about everything—buildings, cars, animals, even people. Everything looked brighter, especially the sky. Was he still in the spirit walk, or had he drifted to another spiritual plane? He tried to listen for the Spirit to speak. Nothing came. Still, he encouraged himself with the assurance that the Spirit would be with him always.

D parked his car in its usual spot. He locked it, and walked toward the building where he kept his equipment. He tried not to appear awkward, especially when he said his morning greetings to everyone he met. *They seem normal*, he thought, so he figured he should just be himself. He found out later that he was nothing like himself.

As he loaded up his cart with his tools, his supervisor approached him. He asked D how he was feeling. Surprised that his supervisor would even take interest in his morning, D responded in the affirmative. He thanked his supervisor for asking and continued to load his cart. As his boss walked away, D heard himself say under his breath, "Fascinating!" He knew that his boss never spent any time asking about his well-being. Was his day going to be like this? Man, only time would tell.

D was assigned to work in a remote area of downtown that morning. The beds definitely needed care. As he began to pull up the weeds and cut off the dead stems, he began to sing. At first, he sang with a quiet voice, but then he became louder. He was singing a favorite gospel song of his. He could sense the anointing, the very presence of God. As he sang, he did not notice the gathering of persons around him. Some even began to sing along with him. When he finally glanced up from his work, he could feel the power of the Spirit lifting him from his knees. His singing became bolder, and so did those about him. The sky had become brighter, and the voices of those singing more filled with the Spirit. He knew where he was. He had entered into the presence of Father.

Shouts of joy and praises unto God rang out from the now growing crowd. More and more came as D became enthralled in the Spirit. He began to speak in tongues. He spoke in Spanish at first and then Mandarin and then other languages of the world. His voice roared like a mighty lion above the voices singing. He could hear others speaking in their native tongues. He knew what this was. It was a church meeting! The Spirit had taught him about this in the spirit walk.

As the Spirit moved about those there, D could sense the call to arms. Spiritual warfare was a serious matter, not to be taken lightly. There were needs that had to be met, and he was the vessel the Father was using. His voice became more authoritative and bolder as he began to call into existence things that had to be. Like the Spirit had taught him, he bound evil spirits and cast them down. He spoke peace into those who had become troubled. He spoke joy into the lives of those who were saddened. He spoke hope to those who were in despair, and he healed those broken in their bodies.

The crowd grew into an enormous multitude. Even so, D knew that where the Spirit was, he need not fear. People were getting delivered! Demons were fleeing from many of their bodies. Healings were taking place, and the joy of the Lord was strengthening the weak. All that mattered was the Father receiving the glory due to His holy name. D knew that time and space was not to be factored into what was happening, for this was what spiritual warfare was all about.

A woman, frail and sickly, managed to come before D with the help of another whom D later found to be her daughter. Recognizing the woman's bloodstained soul, D knew what he had to do. He laid his hand upon the woman's forehead and spoke healing into her body. Immediately, the woman's body became whole. She began to jump and shout praises unto God! Others saw and began to step forward. These were the ones who had shown up recently, who had not received their healing when the Spirit first was ministering. One very old gentleman who was completely blind in both of his eyes came forward with the aid of another man. D looked upon him, and being moved by the Spirit, he commanded the man to be whole in the name of Jesus. Without hesitation, the old man's eyes were opened. He jumped up and down, shouting that he could see again. Praises unto God could be heard from the crowd. Others came forward, and D either laid his hand upon them or spoke healing into them. He was abiding in the anointing of the Spirit! Suddenly, the crowd became still and silent. Their praises ceased as a young boy and his mother appeared. She was pushing him in a wheelchair. The boy had no legs, for they'd been severed because of a bombing in his native country. D knew that God had sent him to minister to any and all people regardless of race or religion. If they believed, the Father would deliver them. As the two approached D, the crowd, now hushed, stood still. In the spirit walk, D had been taught how to use the creative power of God. He knew that it was God's Word that caused that which was unseen to be seen and that which was nonexistent to become reality. D rebuked fear, not from himself but from the fearful hearts of some in the crowd. D leaned forward toward the little boy, laid his hands upon both sides of his face, and looked into the child's eyes. D felt the creative power of the Spirit surging through him like vats of hot oil. With authority, D spoke that the child be made whole and that his legs be restored. The boy shouted! Some thought that he was in severe pain, but when they saw the boy leap from his wheelchair and dance about, they knew that God had restored the boy's legs. Praises and shouting rang out. The boy's mother wept uncontrollably with joy as did many in the crowd.

At about this time the police and EMTs (emergency medical techs) had arrived. When one officer witnessed what had happened to the little boy, he rushed to his squad car and drove to a nearby hospital where his grandmother was dying of cancer. The doctors were preparing to send her home to die for they could no longer do anything for her. Once in her room, the officer quickly wrapped the frail woman in a blanket, picked her up, and started out the door. A nurse asked him what he was doing. His response was quick and to the point. He said, "I am going to get my grandmother the help she needs!"

When the officer arrived back at the place where D and the others were, the crowd had grown much larger. The officer did not have to press his way through. It was as though he'd been expected, for as he carried his grandmother, people cleared path for them. It was as though the Spirit was going before him and making the way. When he finally stood before D, the two didn't make a sound. Their eyes met. D only heard the Spirit calmly speaking to him, "The woman is dead." D wanted to weep, but he remembered his training in the spirit walk. The Word of God was life, and the power of death was defeated at the cross. D leaned forward, first looking at the officer, who had tears coming from his eyes. D then spoke to him, "Be of good cheer. Jesus loves you." He then looked upon the officer's grandmother, and with the anointing, he spoke life back into the woman's body. The officer was so overjoyed that he sank his head into his grandmother's chest. She hugged him with both her arms. The crowd praised God with a tumultuous sound that others could hear for miles. Many started dancing as they gave praise to the Father. The old woman and her grandson looked thankfully at D, who only looked toward heaven. He knew that the glory always belonged to God. It was enough that he was being used as an anointed vessel.

D had no idea how long the meeting lasted. Time as well as hunger and thirst all eluded him. He was caught up in the Spirit, ministering to the needs of God's people. As he heard the singing of faith-filled songs, he knew that the Father was getting ready to end the meeting. With the most brilliant of light, the entire area was engulfed with the presence of the Father. Everyone fell to their knees and gave sincere honor to God. Even D fell to his knees, weeping with joy.

The moment passed. D looked up from his work only to find that he was back where he had started weeding. He looked at his watch, and the time had not passed. He looked around. People were casually walking past on their way to … wherever! They paid no or little attention to D. It was as though nothing had happened. D thought, *That was nothing like what had happened in the spirit walk.* Had the meeting actually taken place? Did God use him to heal and deliver the many he'd seen? And most of all, had the Father used him to raise that grandmother from the dead? He had so many questions. He tried to listen for the Spirit to explain what had happened, but there was no voice. D shook his head and continued his weeding.

Later that day just before D left for home, a strange yet wonderful feeling came upon him. As he walked to his car, D saw one of the women who had been at the meeting. As she walked passed D, she whispered to him, "Thank you." D recognized the witness of the Spirit! He was telling D that what he had experienced earlier that day had really happened. D hurried home, for he had to talk to God.

When D got home, his impulse was to fall to his knees to talk with the Father, only the Spirit led him to the kitchen. D realized that he had not eaten or drank anything all day. He prepared himself dinner and drank some water. The excitement of the day was still flowing through every part of his being like an unstoppable waterfall. As D sat down to eat, the Spirit calmed him down. It was time for understanding. Yes, the Spirit had given D a reality of a spirit walk. The spiritual warfare, the deliverance from evil spirits, and the healings all had happened. When D had spoken to the little boy whose legs had been restored, D had used the creative power of God, which is His Word, and called things that are not into existence. He had also raised the dead, simply calling the woman's spirit back into her body.

D sank in his chair. "Wow," he said and sighed. "Thou art God all by Yourself! Thank You, Jesus, for Your grace!" D now understood why he had trained in the spirit walk. Now he faced the reality of the impending spiritual war.

Chapter 4
Marcus

Marcus had been a gangbanger since he was seven. His dad had been killed by a gang member when he was five. He swore that he would be the fiercest gangster around. He had watched and learned everything about gang signs and the weapons many of them used despite his mother's teachings and their trips to church. His heart was hardened when he saw his dad lying in his blood from a gunshot wound to the head. Marcus just stood over the body, stunned, paralyzed, looking at parts of his dad's brain oozing out. Perhaps that was when the demonic spirits possessed the young boy because he was never the same after that.

When Marcus was a baby, his dad would play with him, bouncing him up into the air ever so gently, catching him and then smothering his face into Marcus's baby belly. It was a tender moment played often between the two. When Marcus was three, he and his dad would play catch with a softball. They'd run about in the house because playing in the yard was too dangerous because sometimes gangs or some crazed neighbor would start shooting. To Marcus, it didn't matter as long as he was with his dad. His mom was there too, but she had to take care of his baby sister, who had just been born. And though he knew nothing about where babies came from, he loved his sister dearly. He couldn't play with her like his dad, so he just watched her when she slept or played in her baby pen and kicked her little legs and arms in the air. The only time that he could not watch his sister was when his mom was changing her diapers or giving her a bath.

Life was okay then. Marcus's dad worked two jobs in order to keep food in the house. Why, he'd even work jobs on the side just to buy those special things for Marcus, his sister, and especially his mom. He seldom would buy anything for himself. That's the kind of dad his father was. Perhaps that was why Marcus took his dad's death so hard. It devastated his little heart. Life was never the same afterward.

Two years after the murder of Marcus's father, he started hanging around certain gangbangers. Oftentimes the gangsters would shoo him away, saying that he was too young. He shrugged them off, telling them many times that he was as tough as they were. He was determined to be a gangbanger. Some thought he wanted to avenge the death of his dad. Whatever the reason, Marcus had an evil spirit prodding him. He learned how to shoot a gun at seven, and he also learned to fight. He could best any boy around his age. He was not only fearless but masterful too. He'd watched the kung fu movies on TV and learned many of the moves. His mother saw what was happening. She tried taking him to church in the hope that he would receive help from the Lord. She often prayed for him, many times crying at night. Marcus would often hear her in the next room. He'd even see her weeping sometimes. He would just snarl, damning her under his breath. He felt that his mom did not love his dad as he did.

When Marcus was eight, he nearly beat a boy to death after he had made his little sister cry. Some who had witnessed the fight later said that Marcus had fought like some crazed person. It took four grown men to stop him. He was placed in the detention home for a brief time. His mother felt helpless. She felt she'd done all she could. Later that night when she was alone in her room and Marcus's sister was asleep in her bedroom, she kneeled at her bed with her face in her hands and cried bitterly, "Lord Jesus, I've done all that I can do. I've tried to help my son. I've done all I thought was right in raising him. I taught him right from wrong." At this point she began to weep more heavily, but she didn't want to wake her daughter, so she pressed her sobbing into the coverings of her bed. "I surrender him into Your hands, my King! He is no longer mine but Yours! Do as You must with him, but save his soul!" At this she lifted her head and focused her lamenting toward heaven. "Father, hear me. I pray! Let Your will be done! For Your glory, my King! In the name of Jesus, I pray." Her head fell upon her bed, and she eventually cried herself to sleep.

When Marcus returned home after three days of detention, he was more determined to rule the streets. Being in detention only fueled his vendetta. No one was going to stop him from being the most fearless and toughest gangbanger in the hood. He wanted all to recognize him and to fear the very thought of his name.

When he walked into his mother's house that day, he didn't even speak to her. Nor did he look at her. She knew that he was angry, so she just whispered a prayer unto the Lord. Marcus looked in on his sister. She was playing with the dark-skinned doll he had given to her last Christmas. He smiled. His sister was the only joy in his life. He thought very little of his mom. He continued to his room and closed the door. Later he heard a knock. It was his mother. "Marcus, do you want anything to eat?" she quietly asked from behind the door.

"No," Marcus growled, trying not to be too obvious. "Not right now." Though he hated his mom, he still had to play the part of a son since he was still living in her house.

"Just let me know when you're hungry," said his mom. Then before she walked away from the door, she lovingly but tenderly trembled and said, "I love you." Marcus only covered his head with his pillow.

There is little anyone can do when a young child is obsessed with such vengeance. No matter what a parent or help agencies try, unless that child wants to be helped, he or she cannot be helped. Marcus was such a child. Each year he perfected his hatred and vengeance. He proved himself to be the top dog of his age group and even to the gang leaders. Some had given him a gang name, but he despised it. When one gang member shouted his gang name, Marcus pulled out his knife like a flash of lightning and slashed the gangster's throat. Marcus was thirteen, and the boy he'd cut was nineteen! Marcus did not care. He hated gangster names. His dad had named him Marcus, and Marcus was his name. After the incident the hood saw him in a different light.

After the knife incident, many wondered seriously about where Marcus's life was headed. Though the nineteen-year-old had survived the slashing, many felt that it was just the beginning of a more downward spiral for the youngster. They were correct. Marcus was sent to the detention home for the umpteenth time. His mother and sister only could stand back and watch him destroy himself. They'd pray often for him, for both loved him dearly. The church they attended faithfully also prayed for him. His sister often cried because of what she saw happening to her big brother.

Whenever Marcus was placed into the detention home, he would learn new skills, all which were bad. He'd learn how to fight more effectively and how to steal more cunningly, and he also learned the best ways to kill. The home was a bank of knowledge for gangbangers and crooks. It was a system that could not and did not help young people, especially black boys of his age. He learned not to care for whites, even though his mother had taught him better. He had fallen into that cesspool system where hope was never an option. He knew that his life would be short. Still, his desire to find the one who had killed his dad grew stronger each day.

CHAPTER 5
Marcus's Demise

During his latest time at the detention home, Marcus had been approached by an older thug. He told Marcus that his exploits had been noticed by some of the hood's most powerful gangsters and that he wanted Marcus to meet with them when he got out.

"What do they want me for?" Marcus asked.

"To offer you a job. And by the way, my name is P-Boy." P-Boy extended his hand to Marcus as a gesture of friendship. Marcus looked him up and down, trying to see what this dude was really about. He looked at P-Boy's outstretched hand but would not shake it.

"I don't go out for gang names," said Marcus. "My name is Marcus. What's yours?"

"There's a lot in a name," answered P-Boy as he slowly withdrew his hand. "Gangster names tell what you really are."

"So what does P-Boy mean?" Marcus asked, not really interested.

P-Boy kind of smirked, almost feeling a bit ashamed to answer. "My name doesn't matter," he finally answered. "What's important is what you want to do once you leave this place. You want to make plenty of cash, drive the best of wheels, hang with the flyest of hotties, don't you?" P-Boy paused so that Marcus could view the picture. Then he continued, "Or do you want to die in your pool of blood from some other gangster's gun? The people I work for can give you all the good things you desire. All you have to do is ... check them out."

Marcus looked into P-Boy's eyes. He had the skill of knowing whether a person was for real or not just by looking into their eyes. It was something he'd learned from his dad. P-Boy looked away from Marcus's stare. Marcus now knew that something was not right. "What's the real reason you came to talk with me?" Marcus asked.

Though older, P-Boy was a bit scared of Marcus because of the reputation Marcus had made for himself in the hood. Everyone had heard about his many fights and how strong he was when he beat down someone. P-Boy backed up. "Look, dude, I'm just the messenger," P-Boy carefully answered. "I've got nothing against you. I don't care whether you go see my boss or not." P-Boy wanted to appear like some bad gangster as he awkwardly started to walk away. For a moment Marcus thought, *What the heck! I'll see what this dude is all about.*

"Okay, man, I'll check it out. I have four more days here. When do you leave?" Marcus finally asked.

"I leave tomorrow," answered P-Boy. Then he looked around to see if anyone else was looking. He reached into his pocket, got out a folded piece of paper, and handed it to Marcus. "This is where you need to go and the time." P-Boy handed Marcus the paper. Marcus took it quickly and scanned it before putting it into his own pocket. "Like I said, my boss has had you on the radar for a while. You'd be good for the business."

Marcus didn't like this, but he knew that if he wanted to find the man who'd shot his father, he'd need money. "Later," Marcus told P-Boy as he walked away. Since detention inmates were separated according to age, Marcus knew that he would not see P-Boy after that day—at least not in the detention home.

When Marcus got out of the detention a few days later, he did not want to return home. He knew that looking at his mother would be difficult, and it would be even worse looking into the eyes of his baby sister. He was supposed to be protecting her from the thugs and sexual predators of the hood. She was getting into that age where the predators would want to lay with her. Still, he was being pushed by a hunger that had to be satisfied. Vengeance is an unhealthy feeling that can leave a person void of humanity. It eats away the soul little by little until all that is left is an empty shell. He knew this, for he'd heard his mom and the preacher tell him often enough. But that didn't matter. His path was fixed. He had to avenge the death of his dad.

When he arrived at his mom's house, Marcus stopped just before knocking. It was afternoon, around two. He still didn't want to see either his mother or his sister. He turned around and headed back down the street. As he walked, he took the piece of paper given to him by P-Boy. He stopped near a storefront wall where no one could easily see him and carefully read the note. For a troubled boy, Marcus was not an uneducated youngster. He'd paid attention in school (whenever he went) and had learned many things just by watching others and TV. His mind was absorbent like a sponge that soaked up anything that he felt was usable in his quest to avenge his father. He read the note to himself. It said that he was to come on Friday at one o'clock in the afternoon. Today was Wednesday. He thought to himself that if this so-called boss really wanted his skills, he would see him anytime. Marcus decided to go to the address on the paper right then, although he didn't know exactly where the building was.

As he walked down the street, he could feel the eyes of those standing on the corner burn into the back of his neck. They were lowlifes, mostly drug dealers and thieves. He cared little for them, for such snakes only cared for themselves. Yeah, he had ethics, but they were his ethics! He walked several blocks, turned a number of corners, and crossed a few streets until he finally came to the building. It was a huge office building located near downtown. He hadn't realized that he'd walked so far. He opened the fancy door to the building, stepped inside, and marveled at the building's decor inside. He'd been to several such places with his mom, mostly to pay bills and such, but this … well, this felt different. Who would be handling a business like this that would want his skills? He wasn't what you might call a hardened criminal. He hadn't killed anyone … yet! The instructions on the note said that he had to go to the top floor. At age thirteen his experience was a bit more advanced than many of his peers. Good thing he'd paid attention to the many movies and TV shows.

When Marcus stepped off the elevator, he saw in front of him two well-dressed black men. They looked like they were seasoned killers. Any normal person would have been intimidated, but not Marcus. He had been called. Besides, he had little fear of death. One of the men approached Marcus.

"Why are you here?" he asked in a threatening voice.

"I'm here to see your boss," answered Marcus, reaching into his pocket and handing the man the note. The thug opened it, looked at what it said, and walked back toward the door where the other thug stood guard. Marcus tried to follow, but he was told to wait. Marcus stood still with his eyes fixed upon the other guard. He looked the thug right in the eyes, not fearing him at all. It was like a stare down, only Marcus knew what he was seeing. Marcus was using the technique his dad had taught him about sensing the thoughts of others just by looking into their eyes. Perhaps this was why he didn't like looking at his mom or his sister. He always sensed their hurt and pain for him.

Soon the other thug came back out into the hall. He gestured for Marcus to enter the room. As Marcus stepped into what looked like a very large room with several doors, he could not help but be fascinated. He'd never seen such a place. Later he would discover that it was a penthouse. He was led to another room that appeared to be an office. Several men and three women were there. Some were black, but most were white. He saw a well-dressed white man sitting at a very large ornate desk. *He must be the boss*, he thought. As Marcus slowly walked toward the desk, the others stepped to the side. He could sense the evil about them. He'd gotten used to the smell. When he almost reached the desk, some white dude reached out his arm and stopped him. Then the boss said, "Didn't you read the note P-Boy gave you, or can't you read?" The boss's joke drew loud laughter from the others.

"I read it," quickly responded Marcus. "I figured that you wanted to see me ASAP, especially since you went out of your way to find me. So here I am." Marcus sounded like he was not impressed by those around him or this white man who was supposedly the boss.

"You have no respect, you little punk," snapped a black thug near Marcus.

Marcus turned to the man, and without fear, he said to him, "I know who you are. Why, you're nothing but a bootlicker! Everybody in the hood knows you."

The black man stepped forward, "You little ..."

Marcus simply stood his ground, not flinching at all from the man's threats. The boss then spoke up just before the black thug got in

Marcus's face. "That's enough of that," he chided. "This young man is our guest. Are you hungry ... thirsty?" the boss asked, trying to calm the tension in the room.

Marcus turned from the black thug and looked directly into the eyes of the boss. He knew that this white man was nothing more than a leech, stealing from those struggling in the hood. Marcus wasn't stupid. Yet he had to master the game. "Nothing. Thank you," answered Marcus calmly.

The atmosphere remained tense, but all focus was now on Marcus. He stood before the boss's desk, and he almost looked as if he was the one in charge. What spirit was driving him? Did he really have a death wish as so many had warned? He shook off such thoughts and waited for the next volley from ... whoever!

The boss rose from his chair, walked around to Marcus, and leaned upon his desk. He wanted to appear as the alpha in the room, for he was taller than Marcus. Marcus only stayed calm and assuring. He did not fear what was to come next because it did not matter. If this was the only way to find the help he needed to avenge his dad's death, then he would have to suffer through. The white man looked Marcus up and down. He could sense that Marcus did not fear him, unlike the other blacks who worked for him. This boy was different. Either Marcus was a stupid fool, or he truly had a death wish like the boss had been told. "You arrogant little n—" the boss stopped himself from saying the word *nigger*, fearing that the other blacks in the room would be offended. Instead he smiled devilishly. "I like your tenacity," the boss continued. "When I was told about you, I had no idea that you were so ... young. You've built for yourself an amazing reputation. I can use a young man like you." He then walked to the side of Marcus like some predator sizing up its prey. Marcus stood still, but he was ready to pounce in defense if needed. He could feel his blade in his pocket, and he knew he'd have to be quick if he needed to use it.

The boss walked back behind his desk. He summoned one of the black men nearby. He whispered something in the man's ear. The man quickly left the room. Marcus continued to keep his eyes on the boss because he did not trust him at all! He kept his ears focused on the others, especially those behind him. If something was to go down, he'd be ready.

"I would like to offer you a job. Marcus, is it?" asked the boss.

Before Marcus replied, he turned his head to eye the others in the room. "That's my name," he finally replied.

"The job I have for you is not an easy one," said the boss. "In fact, there's a learning curve involved."

"What's the job?" interrupted Marcus.

The boss was a bit uneasy. He'd never met a youngster like Marcus. "It's pushing some product for me and my associates."

"You mean drugs," said Marcus. "I don't do drugs. Nor do I push drugs, especially in the hood."

The boss became a bit irritated now. He was the boss of an organization that spanned several cities and had hundreds of blacks working for him. How dare this … this punk deny him! Though he was angry, the boss knew that he had to stay cool, or the others in the room would see his weakness. "What exactly did you think I called you here for then?" he asked Marcus.

"I was told you wanted to see me and that you had checked out my skills. Again, I don't push drugs." Flashes of Marcus's dad ran through his head. His father had often told him how drugs had destroyed many lives in his community. Many had died of overdoses, while many had been killed because of drug crimes. He also remembered that his dad had been killed because he had stood up to the drug dealers.

"Okay," the boss responded. "I can still use you. Step outside into the other room while my associates and I discuss your future."

Marcus slowly turned around, staying alert because anything that could happen. He walked out into another room as someone closed the door behind him. There were three black dudes and one white chick who was dressed like someone's sex doll. He knew about such women. His mom had taught him well. He didn't want his baby sister to look nor to act like such. He hated such women! He sat down, still staying alert but not fearing what might happen. It was as though some invisible force was guiding him, keeping him calm and focused.

It was a few minutes later that Marcus saw P-Boy enter into the room and walk passed him. He was with a white man dressed in some very expensive clothes. Marcus looked right at P-Boy, only P-Boy ignored his gaze. Marcus could only wonder what was happening in the next room. He only could hear muffled sounds. Whatever was going on, he felt an uncanny feeling about it. He was fascinated about just how cool he was. It felt as if he was not there alone. Sure, there were the gangsters in the room with him, but what he felt was something different. He did not recognize it, but the feeling felt assuring, even comforting.

Thirty-five minutes later, the door to the boss's office swung open. One of the thugs who had been in the conference commanded Marcus to come in. Everyone seemed satisfied about whatever had taken place. Some smiled too obviously, while the others, mostly the blacks, just looked blank-faced. Marcus calmly walked up to the boss's desk and stood confidently.

"My associates and I have decided that we like you and that we would truly like for you to be a part of our organization." Then the boss looked at P-Boy before he continued, "P-Boy here has been scouting you for a while and has convinced us that your skills could be used to solve some of our ... let's say troublesome problems. It won't involve you selling drugs, but it will help our bottom line tremendously. Do you understand?"

Marcus looked first at P-Boy, who looked terrified. What had he discussed with them about him? Marcus shook off the thought before he answered, "Yeah, I understand."

"Good," the boss said. "We need to first see how you can handle yourself before we seal any deal. P-Boy will take you to where you need to go. There, you will receive a small suitcase. You have to bring it back here and hand it to me ... and only me. Understand?"

"Yeah," answered Marcus, again looking at P-Boy. Everyone simply nodded their heads in agreement. Marcus and P-Boy started out the room. Still, Marcus could not help but feel that something bad was afoot. He could sense that what was about to go down was not good. Then a thought gripped him. What if he was picking up drugs? What if he got caught by the police and accused of drug-peddling? He knew by the conversations in the hood that blacks got serious time in prison. He'd also heard that many would go in as men and would come out fagots. When he and P-Boy got outside and walked around a corner, he stopped and placed his hand to P-Boy's chest, all the while touching the blade in his pocket.

"What's up, P-Boy? What was discussed about me in that room?"

"Man, why are you sweating me?" P-Boy answered nervously. "The boss gave you your marching orders. I don't know anything else."

Marcus somehow knew that he was lying. "If drugs are in that suitcase, you're a dead man," Marcus said as he showed P-Boy the handle of his knife in his pocket.

"Naw, man, it's not like that!" P-Boy said, shaking and slightly peeing in his pants. "The boss knows you don't want to push drugs. H … he's down with that."

Marcus eased off, but he stayed alert. He just had a feeling that all was not well. They continued to walk a bit until they came to a car. Another black thug sat behind the wheel. P-Boy told Marcus to sit in the back as he got into the passenger's seat. They drove several blocks and across a bridge into a part of the city that was unfamiliar to Marcus. He felt like that dog in a book he'd read. Its owner had taken it far from its home only to leave it stranded, hoping that the animal would die or be killed by a predator. Was this what was happening to him? He stuck his hand again into his pocket and gripped his blade. *Yeah*, he thought. *I brought a knife to a gunfight!*

When they finally arrived to the designated place, Marcus had settled in his heart that what was to be … was to be. He was told to get out of the car, ring the bell on the door, and tell who answered that he'd come for the package. "They know you are coming," said P-Boy.

Marcus closed the car door behind him and walked to the door of the house. It was a very large house that must have had several bedrooms and baths. He figured being so far out from the city, there must have been a swimming pool too. He rang the doorbell. Seconds later a tall, slim white man answered the door. "I believe you are expecting me," said Marcus, showing no fear.

The man motioned for him to come into the house and then closed the door. Marcus could hear tires spinning out. The thought came to him that P-Boy and his ride were gone! When he realized that he was in a trap, he closed his eyes and briefly saw his dad smiling.

CHAPTER 6
Irony

Very seldom do days in the city, especially in the hood, look so refresh and inviting. It was such a day. Children were standing and waiting for the school bus, supervised by some concerned parents because they knew drive-bys could happen at any time. Vendors were early to open their shops. People were catching the city buses on their way to work. It definitely looked like an abnormal day. Life always tended to give you a curve, especially in the hood.

It had been six years since anyone had seen or heard from Marcus. He would have been nineteen now. His sister, now sixteen, was in high school. She was one of the kids standing at the school bus stop. Her life up to then had been fairly uneventful. Most of her peers knew that she was the sister of Marcus, and though no one had heard or seen Marcus for six years, his reputation was legend in the hood. Marcus's sister had stayed out of trouble. She was a model student, studying hard to maintain her honor roll status. Her mom was so very proud of her. She often helped her mom at the church and volunteering in the community. She read to the elderly at one of the senior centers. She loved helping others. Still, each night she'd pray for Marcus, hoping that he was safe.

When Marcus's sister was born, it was Marcus who had suggested her name. He'd wanted his parents to name his sister Brenda. When asked why, Marcus could only reply that he liked that name. He later found out that the name Brenda meant sword. His little sister was a sword. How ironic! Brenda didn't try to fit her name. She just was. She excelled in all that she did. Though she did not participate in school sports, she was a whiz on her debate team, and she could sing with the best voice. Some even said that whenever she'd sing, her voice would cause joy to rise up in the soul, especially when she'd sing in her church. Her mother was indeed very proud of her.

When she got to school that day, she overheard a student talking about a new young player in the gangs. At first, she paid little attention to what was said—that is, until the boy mentioned that the gangbanger had a funny-looking birthmark on the back of his right hand. She couldn't help herself as she walked over to the boy and asked about the mark.

"What did the mark look like?" Brenda asked, interrupting.

The boy did not know Brenda. He eyed her at first. "Who you?" the boy asked.

"What did the mark look like?" Brenda asked again, only more urgently.

"It looked like a question mark," said the boy.

"Where did you see him?" Brenda asked.

"Hey, I don't know you! I could get in trouble, and I ain't about to—"

But before the boy could finish, Brenda cut him off. "Where?" she asked, this time demandingly.

Fear gripped the boy as if something had over taken him. "I saw him getting out of a car near the pool hall," the boy answered in a shaky voice.

Though Brenda was a bit late for class, she rushed to a secure place to call her mom on her cell phone. Had the boy seen Marcus? Marcus had such a mark on the back of his right hand, only her mom had said that it was a sickle. Her mom was speechless as Brenda related the boy's story of the sighting. When the phone went silent for a minute, Brenda thought that she'd been disconnected. "Mom, are you still there?" she asked. When she looked at her phone's face, she noticed that she was still connected. "Mom … Mom, are you there?"

Her mother finally answered, sobbing but there. "I … I'm just a bit shaken, baby," said her mother.

"The boy said that the boy he saw had a birthmark similar to Marcus. It could be him, Mom," Brenda said. But Brenda's mother only stayed silent. Her mom had cried many times, even crying herself to sleep. She missed Marcus and loved him in spite of his troubles.

Marcus was that which reminded her most of her late husband. Oh, how she loved her late husband! They'd been deeply in love since that first day they'd met. Something about his eyes fascinated her. He was not like the other men who had tried to date her. He came straight and true, not some jive player with a flashy conversation. To her, they were all like plastic people—not real! But her late husband was the throb of her heart, and she saw him every time she saw or even thought about Marcus. She responded back to Brenda, a bit choked up.

"Marcus has been gone for six years, Brenda. Remember, the last report said that he'd been murdered."

"Yeah, but his body was never found," Brenda tried to assure her mom.

"Baby, I have to get back to work. We'll talk about this later," said Brenda's mother.

"But—" Before Brenda could finish her sentence, her mom cut her off. She knew just how painful her mom felt. She remembered the many days and nights her mother had cried out to God for strength and for the safe return of Marcus. Hope had waned for her mother, for her mom had suffered the loss of both of her most tender of loves. Still, Brenda felt hopeful. She, too, often prayed for her big brother, for he was very dear to her as well. Realizing that she was late for first period, she hurried off to class.

The rest of the day was filled with thoughts of her son, Marcus. Marcus's mother worked as a baker at one of the popular stores. She baked some of the most delicious cakes and pies around, but her biscuits were what everyone ordered. She fixed her biscuits differently from anyone else. They always came out fluffy and soft with just the right amount of brown glaze on the top and bottom. Customers often bought her biscuits as stand-alone items. They were that good! And though she did not disappoint her customers that day, she could not help but think about Brenda's call. She became a clock watcher that day, trying to hurry time so that she could get off and hurry home. Could it be true that Marcus was alive? Had the report of his death been untrue? She prayed within herself, trying not to upset her customers, for surely many of them would not understand.

When Brenda got home from school, she made some calls. She looked up the number to the pool hall the boy had mentioned and called. She asked whether there was a young black man there with a birthmark on the top of his right hand. The person on the other end of the phone was suspicious, thinking that Brenda was some cop or worse. Of course, Brenda shouted to herself. No one in the hood wanted to inform on thugs. But she had to know. How could she find out? Her mom would never let her go down there, especially this late. She had to find out whether the boy with the birthmark was her brother. Perhaps she could call down to the police station. *Nuts!* she rebuked herself. They'd ask too many unnecessary questions, questions that she didn't want to answer. *But who would know?* she thought. She sank down in her chair, fighting the hopelessness. And when it seemed that nothing could be done, she remembered a church friend of hers who missioned for the homeless and others. Perhaps he could help her find out. She quickly searched for his name in her address book. There the number was, but would he be available? She had to try. She punched in the number on her cell phone. It rang. With bated breath, she waited for the pickup.

"Hello," said the voice on the other end of the phone.

"Aw, yes, is this Brother Terry?" Brenda cautiously asked.

"Yes, it is," he replied. "Can I help you?"

"This is Sister Tolbert. Do you remember me?"

"Of course. What is it that I can do for you?"

"I was wondering if you can do me a big favor. It's nothing illegal." Then Brenda stopped herself. "I mean, it's nothing that will get you into any trouble, I hope." Brenda clamped down on her lower lip with her teeth, hoping she hadn't scared Brother Terry off.

"I hope not," replied Brother Terry. Then there was a brief moment of silence that seemed like a forever. "Well, what is it that you need from me?" asked Brother Terry after the long pause.

"Do you still minister down by the pool hall?" asked Brenda.

"Yes, I do," answered Brother Terry. "In fact, some others and I are getting ready to go near there in a few. Why? Did you want to come?"

Brenda was fighting back her excitement, but she knew she had to be careful. "Uh, no. I can't come right now. My mom has not come from work yet."

"Okay, what is it then?" asked Brother Terry, trying his best not to sound uneasy.

"I just wanted to know whether you'd seen a young black man around nineteen with a birthmark of a sickle or such on the back of his right hand," Brenda said, almost bursting with anticipation.

"Hmmmmm … can't say that I have. But maybe one of the other brothers has. Do you want me to ask them?"

"Would you?" Brenda said, shaking with the possibility of hope.

"No problem," Brother Terry replied. "I'll give you a call if I find something. I've got your number on my caller ID."

"Thanks," Brenda said, breathing a sigh of relief. "I'll be praying that you are successful."

"God bless," Brother Terry said as he disconnected the call. Brenda also hung up, but immediately, she fell to her knees, praying that the young black man was Marcus. She was beyond hope. She was hoping against hope! She prayed so earnestly that she forgot the time. When her mother entered the house, she found Brenda deeply involved in her prayer. Her mother stood and watched for a moment and then turned toward the kitchen. When Brenda finally finished praying, she heard her mother in the kitchen. When she saw her mom, she realized her mom was quietly praying as she prepared dinner. Brenda didn't dare interrupt, for you just didn't do that when someone was talking to God. She'd have to wait until her mom was finished.

The word that had spread throughout the hood said that Marcus had been killed by some gangbangers. Others had it that he had been murdered by one of his friends. Whatever the story, Marcus was said to be dead. Brenda never accepted any of them, for she believed that God had answered her prayer that very day when she heard Marcus was dead. She had asked God to let the rumors be false and that her brother was still alive, even believing as much during the six years that followed. She was steadfast in her faith, believing that God was bigger than death itself.

When Brenda's mother had finished her walking prayer, it was about time for dinner. Brenda's mom called her into the kitchen to eat. Brenda was ready to share what she hoped was good news. After the blessing of the meal was said, Brenda let her excitement out. "Brother Terry is going to check out that black man with the birthmark!"

"Okay," her mom said.

"It's exciting, Mom. Don't you think?" Brenda was so excited that she failed to see tears begin to run down her mom's face. "Mom, I'm sorry. It's just that I've been hoping and praying for so long."

"I understand. Me too," her mother said, wiping some tears from her face. "It's just that this might be just another dead end."

"Or this could be the answer to our prayers!" Brenda was full of excitement, but she understood all too well just what her mother had been going through. She decided not to speak about it anymore, at least not until she'd heard from Brother Terry. They both sat eating in silence, but it was obvious that hope was on both their minds.

Brother Terry's call came late that evening, almost near Brenda's bedtime. When her phone rang, she quickly grabbed it to answer. "Hello," she awkwardly said.

"Yes, this is Brother Terry. I'm sorry to call so late—"

"Oh, that's okay," Brenda interrupted hoping desperately for good news.

"Yeah, one of the brothers said that he saw a young black man who had such a birthmark that you described, but he only had a glance at seeing it."

Almost hysterically, Brenda asked, "Did he see where the man went?"

"He said that he got into a car and they drove off."

"But which direction did they go?" asked Brenda.

"Sister Brenda, the car the black man got into was one of those fine, expensive cars that … that big-time pushers have."

Brenda was a bit struck with fear and doubt, but she was determined to believe God. "But did your friend say which direction the car went?"

Brother Terry was starting to figure out the reason Brenda was so interested in this young black man. "Sister Brenda, it couldn't have been your brother. Please receive the closure that your brother's gone."

Brenda was almost irate. How dare he question her faith! She refused to believe that God had not heard her prayers. If Marcus was still alive, she had to know. Calmly, she responded to Brother Terry, "Brother Terry, I love you as my fellow believer in Christ, and I want to thank you for your help today."

"I'm sorry that I couldn't be more helpful."

"You did well. Thanks." Brenda hung up. She felt a rush of hope streaming through her being. Marcus was alive!

CHAPTER 7
Brother and Sister

Sometimes when you ask God to move for you, it is not always in the way you expect. No one could have guessed the events after Brenda's discovery of the possibility that her brother was still alive. No one! Many believe that God moves in mysterious ways. The truth is that He watches over His people to make His Word come to pass. It's us who cannot fully understand the simplicity of having faith in His Word. People make it seem so complicated and so unreachable! But in reality, it's not complex at all. Such was the steadfast faith of Brenda. She refused to believe that God had not heard her prayers. She was simple in her faith. She believed that God was God all by Himself!

Months had passed since the sighting of her brother. Brenda continued holding onto the faith that it was indeed her brother who had been seen that day by one of Brother Terry's friends. She'd also surveilled the pool hall and surrounding areas during the day, mostly when she was not in school. She kept her search from her mother, who had fallen into a mild depression. The church helped keep her mom hopeful, but the thought of Marcus being alive was just that, a hope to her.

One Saturday Brenda walked near one of the few restaurants that was still open in the hood. It was run by an ex-gangbanger who had gone straight and started a business hiring young people in the hope of keeping them from joining gangs. It was a very nice establishment that catered to the taste of those living in the hood—that is, the food was what most of the people living there liked to eat. As Brenda walked by, she happened to glance into the window. She abruptly stopped. She could not believe her eyes! There sitting in a back booth with his face turned toward the front was a black man who looked like her brother, Marcus. She looked closer. It looked like Marcus, but she hadn't seen her brother in years. Then as if by some divine intervention, her eyes met his. Yep, it was Marcus! She'd know her brother's eyes from a thousand faces! She hurriedly went into the restaurant. Once inside, she felt intense fear gripping her. It was so intense that it seemed to choke her breath. She silently rebuked the fear just like her pastor had taught. When she felt more at ease, she walked toward her brother, not looking left or right but focusing her eyes upon his. She was not going to lose her brother again—not this time!

Brenda found herself standing before her brother, silent but full of hope and anticipation. She ignored the three people sitting with him. She only saw her brother's eyes, and he saw hers! It was an awkward moment. Brenda saw flashbacks of her childhood with him as they both played and laughed together. This was indeed Marcus, her big brother. Marcus broke the silence. "Hi, little sister," he said quietly. "How've you been?"

Brenda felt a bit stunned. She had to get a hold of herself, or she'd miss the only chance to know what had happened to Marcus. Strength came from her spirit as she finally answered, "I'm fine, and you?"

"I've been better. These are my friends." Marcus only gestured toward them, not wanting to formally tell her their names.

Brenda picked up on the vibe and simply acknowledged them with a head nod. She wanted to talk with her brother, and she hoped he wanted the same. She didn't want to be too pushy because she figured that might spook him or cause a horrible scene. She reached into her heart for what to do, and before she could respond again, Marcus said, "Would you like something to eat, or would you just like to talk?"

Brenda was ecstatic! Was this happening?! Was the Lord really giving her the chance to talk to her brother after these many years? She fought back her tears of joy. She swallowed slightly and then answered, "Can we just talk … for now?"

Marcus beckoned his friends to move to another table. Brenda sat down, facing Marcus. At last, God had answered her prayers! *Her mother ought to see this*, she thought. Many believe that God is elusive, but the truth is that He's right on time!

Brenda got comfortable before she said, "I've been waiting a very long time to see you, Marcus. I wish I could give you a big hug like we used to back in the day."

"Let's not go there, at least not here." Marcus looked unsteady as he peered around the room. "There might be some here who must never know that you are my sister. Many still believe that I'm a gangbanger. In fact, let's not talk here." He reached into his pocket and pulled out a notepad and a pen. "Call me at this number around six o'clock tonight, and we'll set up a time and place where we can safely meet."

"Can I tell Mom that I saw you?" Brenda asked when she took the note.

Marcus thought for a moment before he answered, "Do you think that's a good thing?"

"Marcus, she's been worried for years about you. You may think that she does not love you, but the truth is she does. Why, there's no day or night that passes where she does not pray to God for your salvation."

Marcus only looked blank. He no longer had anger toward his mother for not feeling like he did about his father's death. His response to Brenda was thoughtful but assuring. "We'll talk about this later. You need to go now."

Brenda rose slowly from the table, keeping her eyes on him, but he turned from her gaze to look at the table before him. Brenda knew that all was not well. Still, she had a promise that they would later meet. As she walked out of the restaurant, she could sense Marcus's eyes upon her back. What darkness had he gotten himself into? She knew that she could not tell her mom about the meeting, for it could push her further into depression. Yet she also felt that her mom needed hope that Marcus was still alive. As she walked down the street toward home, she prayed within herself, seeking counsel from the Father. He always knew what to do.

CHAPTER 8
The Meeting

When Brenda arrived back home after seeing Marcus, her mom was already preparing dinner, even though it was before three o'clock. When her mom did this, it meant that the night's dinner was going to be special and that someone was coming over. Brenda walked into the kitchen, praying that she had the right words to say. She braced herself before the words formed into her mouth. "Mom, are we having someone over for dinner?" she asked.

"Yes, we are," her mother answered, not turning away from her cooking. "I've invited Pastor Dunn over. We're going to have my special chicken and rice."

"Are you going to bake some biscuits?" asked Brenda.

"Oh, you know I am. That and some blueberry muffins." Brenda loved the sound of that. Her mother only cooked and baked like this whenever she felt joy in her heart, which was not that often these days. How could Brenda now tell her mother about her seeing Marcus? Surely, that would break her heart, especially if Marcus did not show up for the meeting or worse, if he refused to see her. Brenda decided at that moment to wait after she'd met with Marcus to tell her mom. Brenda turned toward her room as she told her mom to call her if she needed any help. Brenda knew from experience that when her mother was happy, she was in her zone and only wanted to be left alone. Cooking and baking for others was like refreshing rain upon her face that was baked off by the hot summer sun. Brenda would wait for Marcus to call.

Pastor Dunn arrived around five thirty. He was not an unattractive black man at all. He was a bit slim and somewhat tall, taller than her mother. He was a widower. His wife had died several years ago from brain cancer. He had three young children—one boy of four, another boy of seven, and a girl who was thirteen. Brenda often tutored them in their schoolwork. She especially enjoyed the girl. When Brenda entered into the dining room, she did not see Pastor Dunn's kids.

"Where are the rest of the Dunns?" she asked.

"Oh, hello, Sister Brenda. The kids are with Sister Tasha." Pastor Dunn looked over at Brenda's mom, who gestured for him to take his seat. Brenda sat down next to her mom at the table across from Pastor Dunn, leaving the head of the table vacant. Her mother had laid out a tasty-looking spread. When she wanted to or was feeling in the zone, she could outdo the best of them. Once they said grace, they all began to enjoy the meal.

The table conversation was sporadic, and Pastor Dunn did most of the talking. Brenda had her mind on the phone call from Marcus that she hoped would soon come. She balanced her thoughts from the call to the conversation at the table. If Marcus called now, how could she explain that she had to leave? Even worse, would her mom even allow her to leave this late? Like always, she prayed within herself for God to move. Surely, He had not brought her this far just to see her go without. That's not the God she knew and trusted.

"Brenda," her mother interrupted. "Pastor Dunn asked you a question."

"Oh, I'm sorry," Brenda said, startled. "I was lost in a thought. What was it that you were asking, Pastor?"

Pastor Dunn stopped eating and repeated his question. "I just wanted to know how you were handling the others on the debate team at school."

"Just fine. Thank you," replied Brenda.

"You do know that the church has an opening for a Sunday school teacher for the youths. I took the time to place your name into consideration."

"Thanks. I appreciate that," said Brenda, noticing the time. It was almost six fifteen. Would Marcus call, or would he just run away? She rebuked such doubt and trusted her faith.

The meal lasted a few more minutes. When Brenda's mom brought out her blueberry muffins, Brenda's phone rang. She excused herself from the table and walked briskly to her room. Could this be Marcus?

She closed her bedroom door and answered her phone. "Hello, is this Marcus?" she asked carefully.

"Yes, little sister, it's me," he replied. "Did you not think I'd call?"

"To be honest, I had to pray that you would."

"Like I told you, you know that I'll always be there for you," said Marcus.

"That you did. Thanks."

"Now about our meeting. Is it too late?"

"That depends upon where the meeting is and Mom letting me go."

"Yeah," Marcus said, sounding doubtful.

"She's with Pastor Dunn right now," Brenda added.

"Oh, so she's finally started dating, huh?"

"No, it's not like that," Brenda said. But in reality, she really didn't know what was going on between her mom and Pastor Dunn. Still, she had to focus on the situation before her. "Just tell me where you want to meet, and I'll ask Mom."

Marcus really wanted to speak to his sister. He had a zillion things to share with her, but he knew it could be dangerous for the both of them. He cautiously told Brenda where to go, and he also told her that she had to make sure no one was following her. Brenda shook with fear at the thought of such a clandestine rendezvous. When she disconnected the call, she prayed out loud, "Lord, help me through this night."

Brenda's mom and Pastor Dunn were washing up the dinner dishes together. She politely asked her mom, "Excuse me for interrupting you guys, but Mom, is it all right if I go over to the library to study? I'll be back before the streetlights are on." It was a rarity that Brenda deceived her mother like this, but the mission was too important. She justified her lying by believing that the Lord was leading her.

"The library?" her mother asked.

"Uh, yes," Brenda said, stumbling, trying to sound convincing.

"Okay, as long as you don't let nightfall catch you," her mom said, turning to look at Pastor Dunn for assurance.

"I won't. Thanks," Brenda said as she kissed her mom on the cheek. She knew that she had to stay believable and avoid suspicion. She always kissed her mom on the cheek when she really wanted something from her mother.

Brenda left the house, taking her phone and a jacket since she figured the night might get a bit chilly later. She carefully walked down the streets, making certain that no one was following her. She'd learn how to do that from watching dramatic movies with Marcus. She never thought that she'd ever need such a skill. She took note of the people she saw and passed by. The place that Marcus had chosen was not very far from her house, but it was still hidden from curious eyes. She felt a soothing comfort as if God Himself was leading the way. It bolstered her faith that what she was doing had been approved by the Father. Turning this corner and that corner made Brenda think that she was an actress in one of the many dramas she watched. Only when she arrived at the designated place did she realize that it was no show. She stopped at the building and looked left and then right. She carefully looked behind her to see if anyone was nearby. She was in an alley that had several doors. Marcus had told her to go to the third door to her left and knock using a particular sequence. *Man, Marcus must really be using his imagination like he had when we were little*, she thought. He loved to do stuff like this. She stood before the door and knocked according to the sequence. She waited. Had she followed the directions? She held her breath. She raised her clinched fist to knock again when the door opened. It was Marcus. He invited her in.

The place where they were was not fancy, but it looked safe enough. Marcus led her to a sofa where he told her to sit down. He sat across from her in a sofa chair. She felt a bit nervous not knowing what to expect. As she looked around the room, Marcus comforted her. "Don't worry. We're safe here. And no one followed you."

"How you know that?" Brenda asked, looking at him.

"Trust me."

"Okay," said Brenda slowly.

"Mom must really trust you to walk the streets alone these days."

"She knows that I won't do anything stupid if that's what you are hinting at." Brenda was a little defensive that Marcus would start with such a conversation. "I've got little time, so let's just talk. Start with where you've been these many years and why you didn't call us."

Marcus leaned forward. "All right. What I'm about to tell you is not easy for me to share. I just want you to stay cool about it and to not judge me too quickly—at least not before you hear the whole story." He looked deeply at his sister's eyes to confirm her commitment.

"I'm not a child anymore, Marcus. I think I can deal with whatever it is you have to tell me."

"Good," Marcus said, leaning back in his sofa chair. "I just wanted to make sure that your head was on right." He always said that to Brenda whenever he was getting ready to tell her some truths.

"I know that a lot of people think that I was killed by gangbangers years ago. What I'm about to tell you is what really happened. Even I found some of what I am about to share hard to believe." He leaned forward toward Brenda for effect. "Brenda, I was murdered."

Brenda looked shocked but stayed calm. Then Marcus continued as he looked down at the floor. "First, I was introduced to this white man who was the boss of a lot of drug dealers. At first, I thought he was offering me a job. I was driven to a house nearly outside of town. When I was dropped off, I knocked on the door. A white man answered, and he asked me to come in. He closed the door behind me, and I somehow knew that I was going to die. It was as though I could sense my death, Brenda, even before it happened. I closed my eyes and waited for what was to come." He looked up at Brenda to see her face. She was calm. She looked as if she knew the story already.

Marcus continued, "I know I don't sound rational, but I'm not lying."

"Okay, just go on," Brenda said to him.

"Brenda, I love you as my sister like no other brother can. I did you wrong when I left you by yourself with Mom."

"What are you talking about? You didn't leave me."

"I'm talking about the many times when I was sent off to the detention home. You needed me, and I forsook you." Marcus said. He looked as if he was going to cry.

Brenda leaned forward, touched her brother's hand, and said, "You were distraught over Daddy's death. We all were. It was not your fault."

"Still, I felt that I failed you ... and Mom."

Brenda realized that it was the first time Marcus had ever shown any compassion for their mother after their daddy's murder. Was this what he had brought her there for? To hear his confession? Surely, there was more, and she wanted the whole story.

"Marcus, what else happened at that house?" Brenda finally asked.

Marcus wiped a tear from his eye. "I was led to a room where three other white men were." He leaned back into his seat and continued, "One tall dude spoke in a very raspy voice. He told me that the boss, the white boss over the gangsters in the hood, did not like smart and sassy—"

"Niggers," Brenda finished the sentence.

"Yeah. The boss wanted me to become history, that it would put fear into the hearts of the other blacks working for him. I couldn't move or think. For the first time in my brief disappointed life, I was afraid." He sighed before he continued, "Brenda, remember how Mom used to make us attend church and how she taught us to pray? Well, at that moment, I prayed within myself for Jesus to save me. It was weird what I felt next. It was like I was taken from my body and lifted above the room!" At this, Marcus became excited and stood up acting out what had happened. "I looked down upon the heads of those white dudes, and I looked at my own. I mean ... me! I saw when one of the dudes kicked my legs from under me, forcing me to kneel. I saw me looking at them, waiting for ... whatever!" He began to cry. His tears were large and streaming. Brenda could only sit and watch as if paralyzed.

Marcus continued, "One of the men pulled out a gun. He told me ... I mean, my body ... I mean me—oh, whatever—that I had to die!" Marcus had become a bit hysterical by now. So Brenda calmed him down by standing next to him and taking hold of one of his arms. He looked at her and settled down. They both sat back down. Marcus took a deep breath and continued, "I didn't hear the gun go off. Nor could I feel the bullet piercing my brains, but I could see it." Marcus put his head between his hands. He wept loudly. Brenda could only look stunned and amazed. Marcus gained control of himself and began to speak again.

"I saw my body fall to the floor. One of the men kicked me in the side. I guess to confirm that I was dead. Brenda, *I was dead!*" Marcus stopped and looked at Brenda with a crazed look. She couldn't look away from him because Brenda, too, felt a bit crazed as if she was in another dimension.

They were quiet. The silence was brief but felt like a forever! Brenda stood up from where she was sitting and began to walk about the room. She was praying within herself, seeking counsel from the Lord. What Marcus had told her was freaky. Still, she and her mother had prayed earnestly for his life to be saved. Even her church had fasted and prayed for him. She had no idea that this could have been the end result. She'd never heard of such a thing as what Marcus had experienced. Not even in the Bible. Could he just be exaggerating? Perhaps he had been drugged by these people and had had a bad trip or something. Her mind was racing, her heart skipping excitedly, and her spirit … Then a thought came to her. God is God all by Himself, and there's nothing too hard for Him! It was a blessed assurance that she quickly accepted. She stopped her pacing to look at Marcus, who had his head buried in his hands, sobbing.

"Marcus," she began to speak, getting his attention. Marcus's head lifted from between his hands. His eyes were bloodshot from crying. He looked at Brenda, awaiting what she had to say. "I think you may have had a spiritual episode."

"A what?" asked Marcus, surprised but interested.

Brenda returned to her seat and faced Marcus. "Sometimes God will answer a prayer in the most unusual of ways. He may have delivered you from a very bad high."

Marcus looked at his sister with a taste of disdain. He didn't hate her, but it hurt him that she did not believe him. He sat just looking at her, and she at him. No one spoke for a long minute.

Then Marcus broke the silence. "If you think that what I just told you was freaky, there's more." He stood up, wiped his eyes, and began to act out what else had happened. "I looked upon my dead body. Yeah,

I was freaking out … big time! But what happened next was something from *The Twilight Zone*!" He stopped to gather himself. "The men in the room became still. No, frozen. It was like time had stopped! I looked at my hands and around the room. I could move. Well, I could float or fly. I don't know exactly. Whatever! All I know was that this black man appeared from nowhere!" Marcus stopped and looked at his sister. She was sitting still as if hypnotized.

"The black man was around twenty or so. He looked very young. He first looked at the three white men and then my body lying on the floor in a pool of blood. Then he looked up at me! Man, when he looked at me floating, I nearly did a summersault!" Marcus had really gotten excited by now. "He knew my name and called me to go back into my body! Before I knew anything, I was getting up from the floor. Brenda, there was no blood on me—none at all. There was only the blood that had already spilled onto the floor! Yeah, you say it was a bad trip, bad dream, whatever, but I know what I saw."

Brenda was stymied about what she was hearing. She searched her mind to understand. She knew of no such experience in the Bible, at least to her knowledge. Why was Marcus telling her all of this? Was he trying to justify his years of being absent from her life? She sat a bit confused, but she really wanted to hear everything he had to say.

"Marcus, have you ever seen that black man before?" Brenda carefully asked, not wanting to irritate Marcus any further.

Marcus looked straight at Brenda as if looking through her very soul. "No, never." Marcus walked around his chair and leaned on it. "That wasn't the only thing that blew me away. It was what he said afterward." He looked at the ceiling as if he was looking for something. "He told me that it was not time for me to die, that God had called me for the war that was to come." Marcus seemed to trail off at his last word. He walked back in front of his chair and slowly sat down. Then he slowly continued, "Brenda, there is a war coming that will precede the final battle."

"You mean Armageddon?" asked Brenda.

"Yes," answered Marcus, looking directly into Brenda's eyes.

"Because of a promise made to our ancestors by God, I ... I mean we have been called to prepare for that final battle."

Brenda fought to believe what she was hearing. Nowhere in her studies of the Word had she read or heard of such a thing. She shook her head. She wanted to believe, but somehow she just couldn't. She prayed within herself for God to give her understanding or to help her to help Marcus.

Marcus sat and stared at Brenda like he knew exactly what she was thinking. He wanted to continue, but he had to make sure that his sister was okay. He stood up and walked over to her and laid one hand upon her shoulder. "Do you have your head on right?" he asked. "Because there is more. Much more."

Brenda looked up at him. Then she looked at her watch. The time had not moved! When she arrived earlier, it was six thirty-five. It was still six thirty-five! Had her watch stopped? Marcus seemed to notice her surprise, so he explained, "Yeah, that's what happened to me too. You're not freaking out. The black man called what we're in right now a spirit walk or some kind of spiritual experience."

Brenda kept looking from Marcus to her watch to things around the room. Was this some kind of different dimension she'd entered? She rebuked that thought, for the Father would never allow the devil to deceive her like that. Still, she was perplexed. Marcus went back to his seat and plopped down. He looked a bit exhausted, but he knew that Brenda had to be told. "You've been called too, little sister. Just like me. Just like mom. That's why I'm here. Evidently, a promise was made by God to our ancestors, and God always honors His Word. Remember He is not like men who often do not keep their word. God watches over His Word to perform it."

Brenda looked at Marcus with a shocked expression. How did he know so much about the Word? She had studied the Bible for years. Why, she remembered how Marcus had played in Sunday school and church instead of listening. Now he was full of the Word. What had happened? Brenda was about to speak when Marcus continued, "I learned all of this ... and more when the black man brought me into a spirit walk. He told me that the time was nigh and that I had to learn quickly what it was that I had to do." Marcus leaned forward in his chair and said, "Brenda, I learned a lifetime of things while there. The Spirit of God taught and showed me many things, things that I was to do here on this plane of existence."

The two sat looking at each other for some time. It was as though they were feeling the other's heartbeat. Much calmer now, Marcus said, "Brenda, I found out later that the word on the streets was that I had been killed. The white men who had thought they'd executed me informed their boss that the job was done." Brenda listened with bated breath. "When the black gangbangers found out what had happened, they quietly ambushed that white boss and all the whites who had anything to do with my so-called murder. Evidently, the black gangsters thought that the boss was hiring me and not putting a hit out." Marcus fought back his excitement as he told that part of the story.

Brenda sat fascinated by what Marcus was saying. But it was what he said in addition that made her drop her chaw.

"I guess the black gangsters didn't like white people killing young gangbangers like me. It was only when I talked with the black man and experienced my spirit walk that I fully understood." Marcus then stood up and walked around to keep his train of thought. "It was all in the plan of God. Brenda, there is a terrible war coming, and it's not Armageddon."

They both froze. Such a thought, indeed, was too great to believe, and yet—

CHAPTER 9
Brenda's Invitation

Brenda had been faithful in the study of the Holy Scriptures. She was proud that many sought her out whenever they had questions about the Bible. Though she was only a teenager, her knowledge of the Bible was legendary. She could best most learned Bible thumpers, even many who belonged to the clergy. Her mom said that she had what they called an eidetic memory. She might have, but she never flaunted it. She made sure that humility was her guide each day, for she'd seen what arrogance and pride brought.

She looked into Marcus's eyes for a very long time. She knew that he was telling the truth. With some reservation she asked Marcus, "What is it that you must do here? I mean, what exactly did the Lord teach you?"

Marcus leaned back into his chair. "Many things, Brenda. Many things." He now looked deeply at her as if looking beyond her. "I did not just happen to be back here, Brenda. I was sent. I was sent for you."

A shiver ran down Brenda's spine. She rebuked whatever fear that was trying to grip her. She prayed within herself for the strength of the Lord. Surely, her brother was not some demon-possessed man who had come to destroy her. She had to trust Jesus on this one.

Brenda finally got up enough nerve to speak. "Marcus, I do not doubt that you have experienced … something, but what happened to you is not going to happen to me."

"Do you love the Lord with all your heart and soul?" asked Marcus, composed.

"Of course I do," Brenda said, controlling a bit of anger. She could not believe that her brother was questioning her faith when it was him who had played in church and who had joined the gang. The very thought almost sickened her. Then she heard a voice that she'd never heard before. It was like someone speaking through a distant tunnel, only the voice was very clear. It only said one word, "Listen." Brenda froze, unable to even speak or breathe. When she did breathe, it was as though the room had transformed! There was a brilliance in the room like she'd never seen before. There were no dark shadows in the corners of the room or under the table nearby. At first, she wanted to scream, but a peace came upon her that was beyond defining. Then she saw a black man standing in the midst of the room! He wore regular street cloths. He had his hair cropped short, and he had a book in one hand. Somehow she was not afraid. She looked at Marcus, who sat smiling and leaning back into his chair.

"Brenda, meet the black man I told you about," said Marcus.

"Hello, Brenda, my name is D." D held out his hand, waiting for Brenda to shake it. When she did not, he took a few steps forward. "Please do not be afraid. I am here to fulfill the will of the Father. Just like I was sent for your brother, I was also sent for you." D extended his hand farther toward Brenda. Almost with a mechanical move, she shook D's hand. "See, I am flesh and blood," D said in a comforting voice. "Let us talk." They both sat down on the sofa facing Marcus.

"I know that what Marcus told you was an extraordinary story, but all of it is true. Many think that they fully understand God's Word, but they only know the surface. I, too, thought that I knew until Jesus gave me the decoder." He stopped to see Brenda look at Marcus and then back at him. D continued, "You see, God's Bible or His Word is a coded book that must have the proper decoder, and you know Him as the Holy Ghost or the Holy Spirit."

Okay, this was freaking Brenda out! She looked over at Marcus who was sitting too comfortably as if he knew what she was going through. This was crazy! For years she had prayed in the spirit and had gotten her prayers answered. Why, look at Marcus. He was a prayer answered! Now this black man was going to dictate her faith? No way! To Brenda, it felt as though she wanted to bust out of her skin. Was what she was feeling holy indignation or just craziness? Before she could act upon her thoughts, D spoke to her again in a quiet voice.

"Remember the voice said to listen."

How did he know that? Brenda thought. *Had he heard the voice too? Man, this is getting weird.* Brenda had to get a hold of herself. Something was going on, but what?

"Yep, I felt the same way as you do right now," said Marcus, sitting up in his chair. "And I had that same look on my face as you now have too."

"Oh, you think that this is a joke?" Brenda shouted, jumping up from her seat.

D calmed her. "No one here thinks that, Brenda. You should have seen me when the truth was told to me, but I didn't have a human contact to consult, only the Spirit of God." D waited till Brenda sat back down. She did have somewhat of a crazed look on her face as D continued his invitation. "Marcus told you about the war that is to come, a war before the final battle, Armageddon. He and you have been called."

"He said that our mother had been called as well," Brenda interrupted.

"Yes, but she has a timing upon hers. I mean, she is not ready yet." D paused as if in deep thought. D continued, "Brenda, you must want to be used by the Lord. He will not force the calling upon you. I felt like you do now, and so did Marcus. But only a willing heart will He accept." D stopped to give Brenda some space to think. "Neither Marcus nor I can teach you what you need to know," D said. "You must allow Him to teach you through the spirit walk because of the time."

By now, Brenda had settled down. She realized that what was being said could be true. She wanted to cry for being such an idiot. She'd ministered to lots of people about salvation, and here she was doubting! She looked over at Marcus, who smiled as if saying, "I know. I know." She had to surrender, but she didn't know how. She thought that she was already saved and filled with the Spirit. What else was there? Then she couldn't hold her tears any longer. They came freely, streaming all down her face like a gulley washer. Her voice cried out with words of praise and of forgiveness. She lost all control of what she was saying, and yet she was still in control! What was happening? She felt herself being lifted up from the sofa. She could hear her voice speaking a language she'd never heard before. She heard herself scream as the language continued pouring from her mouth. She had never experienced such an awesome feeling. Her tears stopped flowing as she begin to open her eyes. What she saw was simply … mind-blowing!

CHAPTER 10
Brenda's Spirit Walk

B renda stood on the banks of a river. She could hear the sounds of strange birds and other animals. She saw fish leaping in and out of the river's waters. She had no idea what kind. She looked around to see what else was there. She was surprised when she turned her back from the river and saw a village of people. They were dark-skinned! She thought that she was in some kind of book like the ones she had read in history class. Surely, this was not real! She heard them speak in a language that she fully understood, but how? How could she possibly understand a language that she'd never heard before? Before she could think anymore, she heard D's voice speaking to her.

"Wonderfully strange, isn't it?" D asked, standing next to her. Brenda looked into D's eyes, which looked comforting and calm. "You're in your spirit walk. Here the Spirit shall teach you all you need to know for the upcoming war. He will endow you with the spiritual gifts you will need to glorify the Father."

Brenda looked away from D, a bit ashamed and a bit honored. Who was she that God would bestow upon her such grace and favor? She started to cry. D placed his hand upon her shoulder. Brenda turned to hug him, and he did the same. They held each other with compassion, D softly speaking words of encouragement to her. When they finally released the embrace, Brenda asked about Marcus.

"He's still at the other place. Be not afraid, for what the Spirit will show you here will last for a lifetime." Then D got a little serious. "I kid you not that your journey here will be an easy one, for much travail will be upon you at times. It is how the Father makes us pure through the baptism of fire."

The baptism of fire? Now that was something Brenda had read about in the scriptures, but she never put it into such terms as D was explaining. Yes, she'd read and heard about trials and tribulations, but she never fully understood why believers had to go through them. She had to ask D a question. "This travailing that I must go through, what if I fail?"

D turned from her to look at the villagers before them. "You won't. You've been chosen. Remember the Father forever watches over His Word to perform it, or more simply put, He does so to make what He says a reality." He then looked into Brenda's eyes with assurance. "You will never be alone, Brenda. The Spirit of God will always be with you. Even when you fall or sin, as long as it is not the sin against the Spirit of God, the blood of Christ is what the Father sees upon your soul."

Brenda began to weep, not for sorrow or pain but for joy. She could feel the joy of the Lord coursing throughout her very being. D must have felt it too, for he began to weep with joy as well. She was unsure about how long they stayed in that moment, for they were in a place where time could not be measured like it could be on earth. D lifted one hand into the air as he said, "Father, Thy name is holy." He then told Brenda that he had to leave her but for her to trust the Spirit, that He was her guide, her teacher, and her Comforter. Brenda closed her eyes to weep some more, and when she opened them again, D was gone. She did not feel fear or doubt but encouragement. She heard the still voice of the Spirit speaking to her from the depths of her soul, "It is time. Let us go."

And so began Brenda's spirit walk.

CHAPTER 11
Understanding

Marcus was sitting in the same chair with the same expression that he had when Brenda had been taken into her spirit walk. It was as though no time had elapsed. Brenda returned standing in front of him, her face no longer looking confused as before. She had much to tell Marcus, and he probably had much to share too. No one spoke for a time. They only showed their silly smiles at each other. Marcus imagined some of the things Brenda must have experienced, for he, too, perhaps had had similar moments. Soon Marcus stopped smiling and spoke to Brenda with a serious tone in his voice.

"So how was your spirit walk? Was it exciting and full of wondrous adventures?" he asked, looking directly into his sister's eyes.

Brenda acted like a shy little girl on her first date. She had so much to tell him that she really did not know where to begin. "Exciting would be a mild word for what the Spirit taught me," she finally answered. "I saw and did things that I would never experience in my present life! Marvelous things that ... well, blew my mind at times." Brenda had gotten excited to the point where she stood up and almost started to dance.

"Did He give you any spiritual gifts?" asked Marcus, stopping Brenda from her excitement.

"Oh, yeah!" Brenda stopped to look at Marcus with a serious face. "I received the gifts of knowledge, of discernment, of tongues, and of healing." She sat down calmly after answering Marcus.

"Such gifts are needed for the coming war," Marcus said, leaning back in his chair. "Brenda, we must prepare, for what we learned in our spirit walks must be used here. I take it that He told you the reason for the war," Marcus said as he looked earnestly at Brenda.

Before Brenda answered, she looked away from Marcus and then at the floor. "Unfortunately, He did. I cried when He told me." Then she looked at Marcus. "Marcus, how can the people of God be so deceived," she asked, not really expecting an answer. "The blood of Jesus is precious, and the spiritual gifts are for every believer. But they still allow themselves to be fooled by the enemy so easily."

Marcus leaned forward as he said, "The devil makes us focus on the things of the flesh—fancy cars, big bank accounts, fine homes, clothes, you name it. When I was approached by the white gangster boss, that is what he offered me. Why, I was even offered sexy women! I would have taken the deal if it had not been for my revenge against the one who had killed Daddy." Marcus paused as if in deep thought. "Brenda, I was in a very dark place. So much darkness can abide in us that it is hard to see the light of the Lord. He had to deliver me from my vengeance before I could accept my spirit walk."

Brenda understood, for her many experiences in the spirit walk had taught her about the many tricks that the enemy used to deter people from the truth. She looked at her brother and felt his pain—pain that he had felt for many years after the death of their dad. She got up from her seat and walked over to him. She placed her hand on his shoulder and comforted him. "I know, Marcus. I loved Daddy too."

Marcus then looked at his sister with a strangeness that she had never seen in him before. He said, "Brenda, the Lord must have known my hurt about Daddy, for one of the things He first taught me was that vengeance belonged to Him and that it was not mine to give. I learned that what belongs to the Father is for Him alone and that it is enough that He gives us such wonderful things."

Brenda looked at her brother with a new respect. Since she had never had vengeance in her heart, the Spirit had not taught that lesson to her ... until now. She blessed the name of the Lord within herself. She realized that her brother had indeed become an awesome warrior.

They both sat and talked for what must have been for hours. They shared each other's knowledge of the war to come, especially the causes of that war. Both realized that though many would be killed, the war was actually a great revival. It would be a worldwide event that would touch the lives of everyone on earth, and the first, who were now last, would be first again. It was like a circle with a designated point returning back to that point to start anew. God is eternal, and He is outside of human time. What is a lifetime to a person is but a second or two to Him. The great revival had to come in order for Armageddon to be realized.

Marcus finally told Brenda that it was time for her to go. She agreed, and they hugged. Brenda put on her jacket and looked at the time. It was still the same time as it was when she had arrived! She thought, *Yeah, God is God all by Himself.*

When the weekend came, Brenda anxiously hoped that Marcus would call or something. She wanted to talk to him or to someone about the Word burning in her heart. The Spirit had not used her yet—that is, not like He had in the spirit walk. Oh, she'd taught Bible study to the youth that past week, but she felt like few really understood the lesson. The Spirit had revealed to her so much, and she was eagerly thrilled to share the Word. Still, she knew what the Lord had taught her that no one could come unless the Spirit was drawing that person. Sharing God's Word just to anyone is futile and useless. It's like a farmer throwing down good seed on ground that has not been broken to receive the seed.

Brenda's mother was up early that day, doing house chores. Brenda wanted for days to tell her about Marcus, but the Spirit led her not to. It was not time. She cleaned the bathroom, washed the cloths, and dusted the other rooms. Her mom spent most of her time in the kitchen. Brenda had a feeling that a guest was coming over later for dinner. When the phone rang, Brenda ran to answer it, hoping that it was Marcus. Before she picked it up, she realized that Marcus would not be calling her on the landline. She answered with a hello. The voice on the other side was not a familiar one to her. The voice asked to speak to Brenda. "Speaking," Brenda said cautiously.

"You do not know me, but I have a message from Marcus. He wants to meet with you in the place you met last time. Can you be there within the hour?" the voice on the other end asked.

Chapter 12
The Gathering

Brenda hung up the phone after she told the person on the other end that she would be there. She figured out an excuse to tell her mom about where she was going. She knew that this was not normal for her, but what was normal these days? Surprisingly, Brenda's mom said okay to her going out, especially since the house was well cleaned. Brenda brought her purse and jacket in case the wind picked up, and then she tidied portions of her hair. She then said good-bye to her mother and walked outside into the brisk autumn air.

When she arrived at the meeting place, a strange feeling came over her. Perhaps it was just her suspicious mind acting up, or perhaps it was the enemy trying to hinder her. She decided to rebuke whatever she felt, and then she stepped forward to give the special knock to the door. Someone else came instead of Marcus. She was a bit nervous at first until she heard Marcus's voice from inside. The young man who answered the door greeted her and told her to come in. There were several people in the room, including Marcus and the three who had been with him at the restaurant. Marcus stood up from his seat.

"Glad that you could come," Marcus said. "Let me properly introduce you to my friends. This is Bobby. This is Miguel, and this is Marlene." Brenda was shocked that her brother had mastered such manners. The Marcus she once knew would have used some gangster slang. She shook everyone's hand. Bobby was very dark-skinned and about Marcus's age. Miguel was a Latino who looked a bit older than Marcus, and Marlene was a white girl who was around Miguel's age. They greeted Brenda with such love and hospitality. She felt very comfortable, but she reserved her feeling of concern about what exactly was going on. Marcus had told her that they'd meet again soon, but was this it?

"I wanted you to meet some of my crew," said Marcus. Brenda felt a little off guard, especially when he said the word *crew*. Had he slipped back into gangbanging? It hadn't been less than a week. Before she said another word, she wanted to hear what else her brother had to say.

"I didn't ask you here just to meet them. We are expecting D to arrive soon." Marcus then motioned for everyone to sit down. "I have told the others a little about you. I'm sorry I could not tell you anything about them until now. Brenda, like you and me, they, too, have had spirit walks. The Spirit has trained them for the coming war as well. Marlene has an unusual background … or what you might call testimony. Bobby and Miguel are ex-gang members. I'm sure that they would love to share what they learned with you. When I heard what they had gone through, it blew my mind."

"Then why did you call them your crew?" interrupted Brenda. "I thought you were back in some gang again."

"Oh, sorry about that. Poor choice of words," answered Marcus. "The four of us have been in training—"

"You mean undercover," Bobby interrupted.

"Okay, undercover. We've been checking out what has been going on in America, how the enemy is really using our leaders to divide the nation. It's bad, Brenda. Very bad."

"You don't have to tell me," Brenda said, feeling a bit ashamed that she had spoken. "But why were you acting so weird at the restaurant? These are the same people here when I saw you."

"Oh, that. Well, we did not want to be seen by the gangs who knew me back in the day. It would have been awkward, especially since they thought that I was dead, especially P-Boy," answered Marcus.

"Then you don't know that P-Boy was killed by thugs after your supposed demise. Now that I think of it, some said that he was killed because he was the one who had set up your ambush." Brenda spoke with a sense of remorse, for she now realized that many had been killed all because of a drug lord's desire to kill her brother.

"It wasn't P-Boy who set me up," defended Marcus. "Still, we had to be discreet because of what we have to do here. Things are bad, Brenda. Like I said … very bad!"

"It's worse than anyone could know," added Marlene.

"It's not just here in the States but all over the world," Marcus continued. "From what we can gather from the Spirit, it's the prelude to that which was prophesied."

"Preachers have been giving the clarion call for years about the end of the world," Brenda interjected. The rest of the group looked at one another, and then they all looked at Brenda.

"Then He did not tell you? The Spirit, I mean," asked Marcus.

Brenda looked a bit puzzled. "Tell me what?"

"Before the end or what is known as the great tribulation, there will be a great war in the spirit realm, one that will touch the lives of many." Marcus became quiet as he looked deeply at Brenda.

Brenda was perplexed, forcing herself not to look stupid. She managed to speak but said with a quiet voice, "I don't understand. I thought there was to be a great revival."

At that moment D entered into the room, or rather he materialized. Brenda recognized him as he greeted everyone there. Brenda knew that her questions had to be answered. She didn't like being kept in the dark, especially when she'd learned so much in her spirit walk. But how was she to ask them when she felt so out of touch? She never experienced the things the others had. Nor had she received their training. Before she could finish her self-shaming, D spoke specifically to her.

"Brenda, the Spirit tells me that you are wondering what skills you bring to this war room. Please understand that what you learned in your spirit walk is all that you will need for the upcoming war, for it is not a war where flesh is concerned but rather the spirit." D then sat next to Brenda on the arm of the sofa. "We are but a few here, but there are many more around the world who have been charged to minister to those who will need our help soon. I have come to answer any questions that any of you might have, for the time is near. The darkness is strengthening itself even as we speak."

Miguel said, "D, in my spirit walk, I met only black people. Why not Latinos?"

"The promise started at the beginning with the first. Now it is time that the first, which are now last, become first again," D started to explain. "Though it may sound simple, that's because it is. Remember the Father is eternal ... from everlasting to everlasting. He is not a Creator that abides in monotony or boredom. No, He is a God of adventure, of diversity. When we look at His creation here on earth, we marvel at its magnificence. Yet we fail to see just how great He really is and just how great He has made us." D stopped and stood up. He walked in front of every one sitting. He had a glow about his countenance. Everyone recognized the anointing from their time in their spirit walks. "The creative power of the Father abides in each of you," continued D as he pointed to them all.

"But I do not have the experience like the others here," Brenda started to say. "I've never been in the gangs, and I never did whatever Marlene did in her life."

"But you were called, and you experienced the spirit walk." D looked directly into Brenda's eyes as if to burn what he was trying to say into the depths of her soul. "The spirit walk was not a dream or figment of your imagination. What you saw, what you learned, and what you experienced ... was very real! The Lord taught you how to discern the enemy, did He not?" Brenda shook her head in the affirmative. "He also taught you how to use the gift of healing, did He not?" Again, Brenda nodded yes. "He used you to create that which was good and beneficial, did He not?" At this, Brenda fell to her knees in tears. She could feel the Lord's anointing upon her. She wept until her eyes became blinded by her tears. She could hear the others praising and magnifying the Lord. The room seemed engulfed with the brilliant light of the Father's presence.

D walked over to Brenda, who was still kneeling but no longer crying. D helped her up by her arm and stood her before him. With the tenderness of love, he hugged her. Brenda felt a bit ashamed but realized that the others were also hugging one another. She knew that Jesus was in their midst. They were having church. She wanted to weep again, but D spoke to her with a very soft voice that only she could hear. "I speak peace unto you in the name of Jesus."

They all returned to their seats except for D, who remained standing. He spoke as though speaking to the universe. "The Father is the Creator. The gifts that He has bestowed upon us was purchased by the blood of His Son, Jesus. It does not depend upon works or a sin count but rather by His grace. You ... we are what we are because of the blood the Father sees upon our souls. We are marked. We are His." Then D looked at them. "Be glad that you have been chosen." He then looked again at Brenda. "Brenda, what you experienced in your spirit walk has fully prepared you for what is to come. In fact, He wants you to see for yourself. Stand before me."

Brenda was speechless, and yet she did not fear. She knew within her heart that God had her safely in His care. As she stood before D, she heard D telling her that the group would be waiting for her upon her return. She could feel the Spirit translocating her to another place. Though she had experienced such a translocation in her spirit walk, this time felt different.

CHAPTER 13
Brenda in Christ

B renda looked around where the Spirit had taken her. It was nighttime, and she could see the yellow lights from the streetlamps. It was a bit eerie at first, but she sensed the comfort from the Spirit. She felt the Spirit leading her to a house nearby. The neighborhood was quiet with only a few barking dogs in the distance. As she walked to the door, she realized that she was looking from another set of eyes. She looked down at her body, and she realized her body was no longer her own. It was another's. What was happening? Had she switched body? It was at that moment that the Spirit spoke to her heart that she was in the very body of Christ. Her eyes were seeing what the Lord was seeing. *How can this be?* Brenda thought. She had never experienced this in the spirit walk. Still, she relaxed her mind and accepted what was happening, trusting the Spirit.

She—or rather Christ—knocked on the door. A black woman answered a bit tearful. Christ asked to come in, and the woman welcomed Him. He knew exactly what they needed as He walked over to a boy around the age of thirteen lying on the sofa drenched in blood. Others around the boy were crying. Brenda sensed a small girl hiding in one of the corners, weeping quietly. Christ looked first upon those weeping and then the young boy. He laid His hand upon the boy, commanded the bullet in him to be gone, and spoke healing into his body. Immediately, the blood stopped flowing from the boy's gunshot wound to his lungs. The boy coughed, opened up his eyes, looked around at his family members, and then peered into the eyes of Christ. He sat up, thanking the Lord for what He had done. The weeping that at first had overwhelmed the family now had turned into praise and thanksgiving. Brenda, too, wanted to shout, but it was not her time. Christ quietly left the house. Brenda realized that her night was just beginning.

The Lord spoke to Brenda as they walked down the street. He let Brenda know that the young black man had been shot by angry white supremacists. It was such a night. He helped Brenda to understand that the state of America—and the world—had come to this. Racial wars had popped up all over. Blacks were being killed by whites, and whites were being killed by blacks. Civility no longer existed, and the age or color of the people being killed did not matter. Brenda witnessed this at their next stop.

When they came to another house not too far from the last one, the shooting victim was a small child of around five. She was a white female. Evidently, she was hit by a stray bullet when the white militia had come through. Brenda guessed that much because the neighborhood was mixed, but the white racists did not know this. The family was huddled around the little girl. They told the Lord that she was just playing in her room when the shooting began. She was hit immediately to her head. Brenda could see parts of her brain seeping from the wound. She'd never seen such a thing before, not even in her spirit walk, which dealt with the lives of the first ones of the Lord's promise. They only had spears and arrows, not such lethal weapons as this child had suffered. Brenda could see that the child was dead. Would Christ raise her up again, which was something she had seen in the spirit walk? Before she uttered another thought, she felt the motion from the Lord toward the child. Christ spoke clearly to the child and said, "Be healed and rise." Immediately, the child's wound disappeared. The little girl rose, and she began hugging her mother. The room was filled with tears of joy and praises to God. Christ turned and walked slowly toward the door, turning around before He opened the door. He wanted Brenda to see something. She saw an aura around that family. They were believers! But what of the other family down the street. Were they not believers? She had questions, and the answer came quickly.

Remember the promise God made to the first specifically that the first would be last and the last would be first? Christ gave Brenda the understanding in an instant that the black family had been part of that promise. But did this mean that all black people would be saved or favored because they were descendants of the first? She struggled to hear the Lord speak to her. He had stepped back out onto the streets. Brenda could hear gunfire in the distance, even bombs going off. They were in a war zone. Still, she wanted an answer to her question.

Looking through the eyes of Christ was both wonderful and strange at the same time. They passed by houses with shot-up bodies upon the ground. Many were black people. *Why did Christ pass them by?* Brenda thought. Then she realized the answer to her question. The promise was made to the believers! Not everyone had believed or had accepted the promise God had made. She then understood why there were so many wars in her spirit walk. The enemy deceives those who yield to his wiles. Only those with the mark of Christ would be spared in this war. Brenda relaxed, and like a passenger being driven in a luxury car, she began to enjoy the ride.

Brenda experienced many wonderful things that dark night. One house had been bombed, but she did not know which faction had done it. Bullets and bombs had no preference, it seemed. Christ stopped at the front of the house and commanded the debris to be removed. It revealed a white woman hugging a little boy and two small girls. Pieces of their bodies were everywhere. A white man lay nearby, and one of his blown-off arms and hands lay clutching a baseball bat feet away. Brenda wanted to cry for the loss of such lives, but she could feel the anointing and knew what Christ was going to do. It was like their minds had become one! Christ spoke life back into the bodies. Each body part connected to its owner. They rose up and looked around at the carnage. When they saw Christ, they immediately recognized Him. They all crowded around Him, hugging and thanking Him. He spoke peace and safety to them. He turned from them and continued His walk down the street, for it was going to be a busy night, indeed.

Brenda felt so comfortable now. She realized that it was never her in the spirit walk doing the miracles but Christ! This is what the Spirit wanted her to see. She did have experiences like the others. She felt confident now that yes, she could accomplish anything in the Lord. It was a revelation that had now been seared into her very being. She understood fully the scripture that said, "I can do all things through Christ who strengthens me." The Spirit had to show her by literally putting her in the body of Christ! She was ecstatic. Suddenly, she was back with Marcus and the others. They were just as she had left them. She smiled. She fully understood her purpose in the war to come.

CHAPTER 14
The War Counsel

D walked over to Brenda. She was smiling with the light of the Lord about her. Everyone in the room knew what she must have experienced. "So what adventures did the Lord reveal to you?" D asked.

Brenda humbled herself so as to not look so proud, for the others must have surely had a similar training. "The Lord made me understand that it is … was not me doing the miracles in the spirit walk but Him through me." Brenda smiled with a big, glowing smile.

"That's the way I felt when He showed me too," said Marlene. "Did He show you the carnage and death from the war?"

Brenda stopped smiling and realized what Marlene was alluding to. "Unfortunately, He did," responded Brenda. "It was not a pleasant sight."

"I saw bodies blown apart by bombs and horrible bullets," added Miguel. "When I saw the carnage, it reminded me too much of the gangs. The enemy really did a number on this country, man!"

D quickly said, "That may be so, but God has never forsaken His people. That's why we are now here preparing for that which is to come."

Marcus sat quietly. He was the only person who had not chimed in. All eyes, including D's, looked at Marcus. D must have known what was on Marcus's mind, for he walked over to Marcus to comfort him. "Marcus, about those men who died when you were to be executed, that was not your fault."

Marcus first looked at Brenda and then the others. He then looked down at the floor. "I realize that now, but—"

"Marcus, God is a killer," D interrupted. "He avenges those He loves."

"Surely, the Lord would not have done such a thing," defended Brenda.

D looked directly at Brenda and then the others and then back at Brenda. "Brenda, as a Bible student, you should know that the Father is love, but He also is an avenger. He protects those He loves like any good father who cares for his children. The scriptures are there, but many fail to understand because they lack the decoder. You saw Christ heal and set the bondage free in your last spirit walk, but many of us here also witnessed the vengeance of God's anger."

Brenda could only sit, stunned. Most of her life she'd heard from many preachers that God was a God of love and that He would never do horrible things to those He loved. No, she could not accept it. "It wasn't God who killed those men," Brenda defended almost in a shout.

The others, including Marcus, stared at Brenda, not with anger but with compassion. She had to understand if she was to be an effective warrior in the days ahead. Time was too short for them to teach her. D knew this all too well. He lifted up his eyes toward heaven and spoke softly, "Father, give Brenda the courage to accept your Word so that she may be the strength of your hands." D then sat down.

The room became deathly quiet for what seemed like hours. No one spoke. It was as though they were waiting for a word from God or for somebody. Brenda could sense the others praying within themselves. She felt a little scared, for she was unsure about what was happening. She rehashed all that she had gone through in the past days—the spirit walks and her walk in Christ. She had always pictured God as a loving God that was not capable of killing. How was she to behave now, knowing what Marcus and D had said? She was between understandings, not sure, not certain! Her entire value system had been shaken. She wanted to cry out for help, but she was too ashamed and too afraid! She earnestly prayed within herself for the Spirit's help. Suddenly, the voice of the Spirit commanded her to stand. Without hesitation Brenda stood up. The others turned their eyes toward her. It was like she was in a trance, not moving and seemingly barely breathing. She was not in a spirit walk, but the Word was pouring throughout her mind.

The Spirit was imparting into Brenda the understanding of scriptures that she thought she knew and understood. She remembered that God is the same yesterday, today, and forever. The Old Testament was God's

Word, but many had misunderstood its message. God slew His enemies then with fire and brimstone. He had destroyed the Egyptians in the Red Sea. God had sent angels to destroy Sodom and Gomorrah. These were not just bedtime stories but His eternal Word! Brenda sank onto the floor upon her knees from what she had received from the Spirit. She wept bitterly. Had the others gone through a similar experience as her? She thought she knew the Bible so well! Then like a shock of electricity, it dawned upon her. The Lord had to make her see that she did not know what she should have known! Now she knew.

The others looked at one another with smiles of relief. They knew that the Lord had revealed His truth to Brenda. Marcus was the first to speak. "Well, little sister, how does it feel to be cleansed from religion? That's all most preachers preach these days, you know."

Brenda knew that her brother was not trying to be cruel, for she now knew that much of what she had known of God's Word had been man-made interpretations. She looked around at the others who looked at her with smiles of joy. Though Christ brought grace into the world, grace did not negate the attributes of the Father, especially when it came to His anointed ones. She remembered the scripture where Christ warned that it was better that a millstone be hanged about the neck of a perpetrator and that person thrown into the depths of the sea if that person offended any of His loved ones.

"There was a lot I learned in my spirit walk," said D as he sat down. "Many of you experienced what the Lord needs you to know so that you can accomplish the tasks before you. I kid you not that the war is quite near and the dangers are very real. You all must become so sensitive to the Spirit that your thoughts must gel with His thoughts. The tricks of the enemy have been honed to the point that many of the religious community think that what they are doing is God's will."

"But hasn't that been true since ... well, forever?" interrupted Bobby. "I mean, people have always believed one thing or the other, especially from preachers."

"That may be true, Bobby," D answered, looking directly at Bobby. "But most did not have the decoder as we do. Many listened to that unholy spirit, the devil, especially preachers who were wrapped up in the desires of the flesh."

"Yeah, I can dig that. My uncle was a minister. He preached things that his congregation wanted to hear or what he thought would keep the money flowing." Bobby looked saddened and angry as he stopped speaking. "If I had been taught the Word the right way, perhaps I would not have joined the gang ... or killed so many people."

D had to comfort Bobby for he saw a sadness trying to overcome Bobby. "Bobby, what happened to you was not a fluke. What I mean is that you were called way before your time in the gang. When I had my first encounter with the Spirit, He taught me that God's grace was so powerful that He could snatch a soul from the brink of hell itself." Bobby's head was no longer hanging down. Nor were his eyes teary. D looked from Bobby to the others in the room. "The Lord showed me in a vision of a young backslider who thought that a witch had bedeviled him to the point that he could not leave her but that he had to do everything she said. He was worse than a puppet on a string. She totally commanded his life. One day a small window of light came upon him, and he repented. What happened next, I cannot say, but I saw him take a loaded gun and shoot himself in the head." The others in the room were at the edge of their seats as D continued, "I saw the soul of the young man nearing the gates of hell. Suddenly, he was taken by the Lord and shown the eternal light of heaven. The Spirit helped me understand that God's mercy is eternal and that He has mercy on those He chooses."

A great sigh spread over the room. Brenda began to tear up again. Marlene started to praise the Lord, and Bobby rubbed his hands as if washing something from them. They all felt the anointing in the room. D looked at Marcus. Marcus caught D's eyes and began to speak, but D stopped him. "What happened to you, Marcus, was similar to what happened to that young man. The Father knows your heart, and He knows that sometimes you feel unworthy. But Marcus, we all do at times."

"Amen. Yes, that's true," the others said.

"Let's not forget that why you are here is not about your works but about the promise the Father made to your ancestors." D stood up before them. He looked seriously at each face. "What Christ did on the cross was epic. Few preachers—or believers for that matter—have fully realized just what Christ did for us. The Spirit one day took me into a spirit walk similar to what Brenda just went through. I remember walking toward a fiery place that was surrounded by darkness. At first, I was afraid. Like Brenda, I realized that I was in another's body. When the Spirit opened my understanding that the body was the Lord's and that I was seeing through His eyes, well, I became at ease. We walked through the dark flames. I felt nothing of the heat. Nor did I fear the cries of the damned. I saw demonic spirits scattered about, some daring while others running for cover. The Lord walked up to what looked like a throne. The demon sitting on it was the prince of darkness, the devil himself! I saw Christ take some keys from the enemy's hand. I now know that they were the keys to death and hell. We walked to a prison. Christ opened up the door. I now know that they were the righteous ones who had died under the Mosaic Law. The place was called paradise, and Christ had come to set the captives free! There are no more souls there now. We then walked back out of hell. When I came to myself, I couldn't help but rejoice in the Spirit. I must have praised God for hours!"

Those in the room had begun to praise the Lord again but only more fervently. Marlene had dropped to her knees. Bobby was dancing before the Lord, and Marcus was hugging his sister. D smiled with a thank-you to the Lord upon his face. He knew now that they were ready. He'd done what the Spirit had wanted. They now knew that it was not by them which the battle was to be won but by the power of the Lord. Still, there was one other matter that had to be resolved. It concerned Marcus and his mother.

CHAPTER 15
A Reunion

D looked at Marcus with compassionate eyes. He knew that Marcus had not seen his mother since he'd been missing for years. The Lord's mercy was now leading D to encourage Marcus to face his mother. D faced Marcus and said, "Marcus, you need to see your mother before you enter into the battle." Marcus looked at D with shock, more surprised that D knew what Marcus was thinking about. The Spirit had been dealing with Marcus for days concerning his mother. If Marcus went to war with such a heavy heart, the enemy could use it against him. Marcus sat down, feeling the eyes of the others upon him. They must have known too. "You must go to your mother and seek her peace," D continued. "She loves you dearly."

"I know," responded Marcus. "But I've said and done some horrible things to her." Marcus lowered his head into his hands, hiding his tears.

Brenda went over to her brother and comforted him. She placed one of her arms around his shoulder, and as she spoke to him, she placed her head next to his. "I know, Marcus, and so does Mama. But I forgave you a long time ago, and I know she has too." She then kissed the top of her brother's head as he wept bitterly into his hands.

The others sat down and prayed silently. They all had to make amends to people they had offended, and it was not an easy task. D sat and looked at each of them, wanting to somehow ease their pain, but he knew that it had to be this way. The battles that lay ahead were too daunting for any ill feelings to linger. They had to be cleansed of anything that the enemy could use against them.

Marcus finally lifted his head and looked at his sister and the others. He knew what had to be done. "Will you come with me?" Marcus asked, looking at his sister.

"Of course I will," answered Brenda, hugging her brother.

"We'll be praying for you," Bobby said, and the others agreed.

Marcus and Brenda prepared to leave. The others walked them to the door with their blessings. When they shut the door behind them, Marcus and Brenda began to walk toward their mother's house. "What if someone recognizes me with you?" asked Marcus.

"Then we'll just believe the Lord will hide us in ... the cleft of the rock." They both smiled, feeling confident that the Father had provided.

When the two arrived at their mother's home without incident and without anyone seeing them, Brenda stopped at the door before opening it. "Marcus, I think that I should go in first and soften Mama about you. She's had a very difficult road waiting for this day."

"I understand," Marcus said, a bit nervous.

"Wait in the hall while I find her," Brenda said as she unlocked the front door. When she peeped in carefully and did not see her mother, she gestured for Marcus to come into the hall as planned. "Mama, I'm back," Brenda announced, waiting to hear an answer to determine where her mother was in the house.

"I'm in the kitchen," her mother replied. Brenda gestured to Marcus to wait for her signal. Brenda walked toward the kitchen, placing her jacket and purse upon a chair nearby. When she entered into the kitchen, her mother was taking a pan of biscuits from the oven.

"Mama, how was your day?" Brenda asked, trying not to be too obvious.

"Just fine," her mother answered as she placed the biscuits down to be cooled. "I've invited Pastor Dunn and his family over for dinner. I hope you don't mind." Brenda's mom turned to look at her. Brenda tried to hide her secret and excitement, but she no longer could.

"Mama," Brenda started but hesitated. She did not want to overwhelm her mom about Marcus, but she had to tell her. "I think that it's best that you see for yourself." Brenda was almost beside herself as she gestured for Marcus to come in. "Remember, Mama, we prayed for this."

When Marcus entered the kitchen, he looked a bit ashamed, not knowing how his mother would react. When his mother saw him standing there, no longer the son she once knew but now a young man—and a very, handsome young man at that—she dropped the oven mittens onto the floor and ran to embrace him. The two hugged for a very long minute. She kissed him lovingly upon his cheeks and then his forehead. Marcus could not hold back his tears as he sobbed openly. Brenda, too, could not contain the moment as she joyously cried. Marcus kept pleading that his mom forgive him as he cried in his mother's embrace. His mother eased her son slowly away from her as she cried and said, "I thank the Lord that you are all right. You need not ask me for forgiveness, for God has blessed me ten thousand times!" She then embraced her son again as the both of them cried in each other's love. Brenda, who could not just stand to look, ran over to them and joined the reunion. Praises and thanksgiving to God rang from their mouths. What none of them could see was the presence of Jesus in the midst of the room. They must have rejoiced for what must have been a very long time.

When the three finally relaxed from their embrace, Marcus was the first to speak. "I know that I should have gotten in touch with you, but I was afraid for one and ashamed for another. I—"

His mother stopped him. "You need not be ashamed. God answered our prayers for you. You are here before me." His mother took one of his hands and stroked it gently. "I had a dream the other night that you were home, and here you are!" She hugged him once again.

Brenda then walked over to the stove to peep in. She noticed a pie was still inside. "Mama, is this pie ready to be taken out?" she asked.

"Oh my!" her mom exclaimed, quickly picking up her oven mitts from the floor and dashing to the oven. She quickly took out the blueberry pie and examined it to see if it was done. It was. She then placed it upon a nearby counter to cool and shut off the oven. She looked at her son and said, "Marcus, will you stay for dinner? I have Pastor Dunn and his children coming over, and I would like them to meet you." Marcus didn't know what to say, so Brenda spoke up for him.

"Mama, there's quite a lot of things Marcus … and I need to talk to you about, and—" Brenda stopped, and so did the others. D had been translocated into the room. Brenda looked at her mother, thinking that she was going to freak out, but what she saw pleasantly surprised her. Her mother didn't look surprised at all. In fact, she smiled like some teenager on her first date. "Mama, aren't you wondering what just happened?" Brenda asked after a long wait.

"No," her mother answered confidently. What the others did not know at the time was that God had prepared their mother for this very moment because of the upcoming war.

D then said, looking first at Brenda and then Marcus, "Your mother has seen me in her dreams. The Father prepared her in dreams while He prepared you two in spirit walks. Remember she, too, has been called." D waited to see their reactions. When he did not notice any surprise reactions, he then walked over to their mother and hugged her in a gentle embrace. "Welcome, Mary. I hope you are well." D stepped back to look at her smiling from ear to ear. Their mother's face was lit up like a bright candle. Brenda and Marcus recognized the anointing! But how? How did their mother receive the Spirit? D must have known the questions the brother and sister had, so he spoke to ease their concern. "I see that you three have a lot to talk about. Sit, and the Lord will guide you all." They all sat down at the kitchen table. At first, they just smiled at one another like little children anxious to tell their secrets. D remained standing. "Don't worry about the dinner or the time. The Father has provided."

As the three began to share their stories, no one noticed when D left. Marcus shared what had happened to him first, and then Brenda revealed her story. Their mother listened with great interest and excitement. Then she shared what had happened to her. She told them how she knew her husband was with the Lord, for God had shown him in a beautiful garden working, something he loved and always wanted to do. She told her children how she had received the baptism of the Holy Spirit one day when she was praying. It was after that that she had begun receiving teachings in her dreams, where she had met D. They all looked at the other with wonder in their eyes. Truly God is God all by Himself! He just doesn't use one or two ways to teach His people, but He employs whatever way to get His Word across. It was a time of jubilation for the three, especially for Marcus, for he no longer felt ashamed or afraid of what he had put his family through.

"Marcus, you don't mind me inviting Pastor Dunn over, do you?" asked their mother.

Marcus did not think twice before he answered, "No, Mama. I don't. I know that you loved Daddy as much as I and that you will always keep him in your heart." Marcus's mother reached across the table and touched his hand. She did not speak but spoke with her eyes. She always saw her beloved husband in Marcus, and she saw him more even then.

The three sat for a little while longer before the Spirit ended their reunion. No time had passed, and most importantly, the food was still hot from the oven. D was right. The Father had provided. They all busied themselves getting ready for Pastor Dunn and his kids. Marcus helped to set the table in the dining room with Brenda, while their mother finished cooking. It was to be a new beginning for their family.

CHAPTER 16
Cause to War

The next day Brenda finished her chores. Marcus had spent the night and was still asleep in his old bed. Her mother had left early for work. It had been a most warm and insightful dinner last night. God had truly blessed. Now Brenda had other things on her mind that she wanted to chew on. She gathered her jacket and purse, walked to a nearby park, sat down on a bench, and began to think about all that had just happened. The sky was partly cloudy, and the wind blew occasionally. She looked at some children swinging and playing in the park while their parents looked on. It was too dangerous for kids to play in the park alone these days, too many drive-bys and kidnappings. The world had truly changed, mostly for the worse. Politicians no longer cared for the people they were supposed to serve. It was all about the money now. The rich and the affluent had the ears of political leaders, dictating what should and shouldn't be. Racial hate was everywhere. Black people really got the worse of it. Never before had people of color been so targeted by society. Prisons were full of them, keeping them from voting, one activist preached. As she looked out among those before her, Brenda began to tear up.

The problem wasn't just in America but all over the world. Things were changing. Expressing concern for one another was no longer practiced. The wars and rumors of wars Christ spoke about were ever so apparent. Thousands were being killed daily all for the sake of some political prowess. Nations that used to care for the humanity of others now forsook that belief to instead embrace a more selfish ideology. It seemed that the enemy had played his best wiles and that many had fallen for them.

Brenda wanted to cry, but she knew that her time was not then. She could feel the tug from the Spirit to move. She walked toward home.

She could not shake off the feeling of sadness about the world's plight. Yet deep in her heart, she felt the hope of the many God had called, including herself, people who were to go forward and deliver many. The promise the Father had made to her ancestors encompassed many more than just her black ancestors, for it included anyone who believed. With that, she felt comforted.

When she finally arrived back home, she laid down her jacket and purse. It was still morning, just before noon. She peeked in on Marcus, who was still asleep. Brenda then walked into the kitchen. She drank a glass of water from the tap, something she rarely did. The house was deathly quiet as if someone had died. No, *it must be something else*, she thought. She yawned and thought that it was a strange yawn. Still, it was Saturday, and she was owed some time sleeping in. She went to her room and closed the door.

Brenda lay on top of her bed, looking at the ceiling. She could not help but think about the current condition of the world, especially climate change. Climate change was a very controversial topic. Some believed it was just a hoax, while others believed it was caused by humankind. Why didn't people see what many of the scientists were saying, namely that man's carbon footprints were destroying the planet. She could not understand why so many prominent leaders kicked against the evidence. She didn't notice when she trailed off to sleep.

Dreams were always something Brenda enjoyed, especially when they left her with a smile when she woke up. When she fell asleep this time, she dreamed what seemed to be a spirit walk. The dream showed her just how the world's climates had changed. Yes, there were cycles like many had alluded to, but such cycles had been exacerbated by the foolishness of humans. God had placed in the atmosphere certain protectors, such as the ozone layer. Man's carbon footprint had destroyed much of it. Then there were the scrubbers, the trees, particularly the forests. They had been created for the purpose of recycling the air. Many who fought against such ideas didn't understand the purpose of the trees. Trees took in the bad air (carbon dioxide) that all animals breathed out, and in turn, they would give people fresh air (oxygen). The destruction of the rainforests and trees were proving deadly now.

The dream showed Brenda how the pollution of the waterways, the air, and the soil also affected the climate. The megatons of garbage and useless artifacts that are buried in the landfills daily also help to destroy the planet. When such items decomposed and seeped into the water table, toxins that such materials gave off affected the soils, the waterways, and even the atmosphere. Yet many denied such a simple problem because of their love of money.

The dream took Brenda to a weird turn. She saw the Father creating the universe! How was what she had seen about climate change related to the creation event? She saw the Father speak into existence things that did not exist just moments ago. Though she was excited to see this, she could feel the tugging from the Spirit that there was much more. God called into being planets and stars. Brenda heard Him call also laws that governed these creations. She quickly shouted out, "Physics!" Had the Father laid down the laws of physics at creation? What did this mean? Brenda had taken a class or two about physics but had never really associated God with such. She had heard her teachers say that physics had nothing to do with God or creation. Then what had she witnessed? The Spirit then spoke to her in His soft voice. He told her that many did not accept the concept of creation because they only believed what they could see, hear, feel, and taste. They wanted empirical evidence. God is the chief scientist, and all others are under Him. The world's scientists are simply trying to understand how God created the universe. They split atoms, thinking that they have found a clue, but God knows much more! The creation is a discovery playground for scientists, placed there and designed by the master scientist Himself. The Spirit helped her understand that God has authored every image that anyone can imagine and every thought that anyone can think. *What?* When Brenda heard this, it blew her mind! She shook with both fear and joy. *Every thought and image had been authored by God?* She trembled to think about the implications. Then the Spirit asked her softly, "Who is God, Brenda, but the Creator of *all* things?" The Spirit made certain that He emphasized the word *all*. Then it struck her like a bolt of lightning. The revelation was sure. She had never shouted for joy in her dreams or even danced in the Spirit, but she did then!

When Brenda finally woke up from the dream, she immediately fell upon her knees. She prayed that what she had seen was not from the enemy. She had to wait until the next time she saw the others for the confirmation.

CHAPTER 17
Prelude to Battle

Several days had passed since Brenda had had her dream about the Father creating the universe. She had shared it with both her mom and Marcus that same day. Marcus only smiled, for he had had a similar dream that same day while he'd been sleeping. He said that he'd never had such a deep sleep and such a vivid dream like the one he'd had that day. Their mother only looked pleased as if she knew something her children did not know. When darkness started to arrive, Marcus told his mother that he had to leave. They hugged as each told the other of their love. Marcus did the same with Brenda. He then told her that they would meet again soon. He then left the house, not fearing who he'd meet along the way, for he was walking in God's plan.

As Marcus had promised, another meeting was called a few days later. Around four o'clock that afternoon, the phone rang. Brenda turned down the TV to answer it. "Hello," she answered. It was Marlene on the other end.

"Is this Brenda?" asked Marlene.

"This is she," answered Brenda.

Marlene sounded like there was a bit of urgency in her voice. "We are meeting tonight around six. Can you make it?"

Brenda thought for a moment. It was a school night, and her mother did not like for her to leave the house during the week. "I'll try," she finally said.

"The meeting is vital," Marlene stated. "You must be there. Trust the Lord, Brenda. He'll make a way."

"All right," Brenda said and sighed, forcing doubt away. "I'll trust in the Lord. I'll see you at six. Later." Brenda hung up the phone. She could sense in her spirit that something bad … or good was about to happen. She strained to hear the Spirit tell her about what was coming.

She had completed her homework and had done her chores, and now she had to trust her mother would understand why she had to leave the house. Her mother would be home around five, which did not give her much time. She did not hear the Spirit at all as she paced, praying for an answer. Suddenly, she heard the key to the front door. It was her mother. Brenda looked again at her watch. Her mother was early. What had happened? Why was she at home so early? When Brenda faced her mom, she was stunned by what she saw. There was a brilliance about her body like that of the anointing.

"Why are you home so early?" Brenda asked.

"Oh, hello, Brenda," said her mom. "I needed to get off early today to bake for the soup kitchen down the street."

"That could take a while," Brenda responded. "Do you need me to help you?" Brenda was hoping that she would say no.

"No," she answered as she placed some packages on the kitchen table. "But there is something that you could do for me—that is, if you've finished all your work."

Brenda held her breath, expecting the worse. "I have. What is it?"

Her mother reached into her purse and pulled out some money. "I need you to run down to the corner store and pick me up a couple cans of pineapple."

"No problem," Brenda said as she took the money. Could this be the excuse she needed to go to the meeting? Then she thought that the meeting might run too long. "I bind that thought," she said to herself. She had to trust God that no matter the length of the meeting, she would be back on time. Before she could turn toward the door, her mother surprised her.

"Be blessed at the meeting," said her mother. "And pay close attention, for this could be it." Brenda was pleasantly shocked. Her mother knew!

Brenda left the house around five fifteen. She knew that she would be early. She went first to the store and purchased the pineapple. She was still early. She continued to trust the Lord that she'd get back in plenty of time. When she arrived at the meeting place, Bobby and Marlene were standing at the door. She greeted them, and they all went inside together. To her surprise, Marcus, Miguel, and D were already sitting down and talking. Everyone was smiling as though some great news was about to be announced. Brenda wanted to tell them what had happened to her in her dream. However, she didn't want to dampen the excitement in the room. Still, she politely said, "I know that something wonderful is up because of the smiles around the room, but I want to share a dream I had a couple of days ago."

"We know," Miguel said, smiling. "Marcus has been telling us."

"Okay," Brenda said slowly but without anger or disappointment, for she now felt as one with everyone in the room.

"You can still share what the Lord revealed to you, Brenda," said D. "We have the time. Plus Marcus could have forgotten something." With excitement, Brenda began as she took a seat.

When Brenda finished sharing about how the Father had created the universe and the revelation she'd been given about climate change, she began to feel that the dream might have been insignificant to the mission at hand.

"I, too, had that same dream," exclaimed Marlene.

"Me too," interjected Bobby. Miguel nodded that he, too, had had a similar dream that week.

"It appears that we've all had the same dream," said D as he sat on the edge of his seat. "That's why I wanted you to share, Brenda. Evidently, the Spirit is telling us something."

"I know that the Word of knowledge is a powerful gift, but what I learned from the dream was mostly about the greatness of the Father," said Marlene.

"True," Marcus responded. "Perhaps it's about just how the world has turned upside-down on itself."

"Yeah," Bobby said.

"But what does the dream have to do with the upcoming war?" asked Marlene. "What does climate change have to do with it?"

Marcus wanted to chime in but thought it best not to. They all looked at D, who looked starry-eyed as if he was receiving a message or something. They were all completely silent for a long while. D blinked and came back to himself. He shook his head and then spoke to the group. "We've all had a similar dream about the Father creating the universe and about how the climate is changing. You want to know how such knowledge fits into what we are to experience soon." D then paused. The others saw his face light up with the brilliance of the anointing. They all knew that the Spirit was speaking through him then.

"God gave humankind the charge or stewardship of this planet. You must understand that before this world, the world of Adam and Eve, there was another world where an angel named Lucifer was the son of the morning. The day would not come without his presence. It was a magnificent world until Lucifer wanted to exalt himself above God, and he convinced other angels to rebel against God. There was war in heaven, and those rebellious angels were cast down to the first earth. It is where we see the dark sighing waters mentioned in the book of Genesis." D paused, took a deep breath, and then continued, "Father later restored this present world that we know as the world of Adam and Eve. Adam's seed was to have lived upon the Earth to glorify the Lord. The thing was that the Father had a plan. God no longer wanted angels but a creation of sons and daughters after His own heart." D looked at the others to see their expressions. The Spirit did not want to explain the connection too fast and shock them. "The garden of Eden was never to be the place where it all ended. It was the place where it all began—that is, the birth of the sons of God. Remember the Father could have easily cast out the serpent and kept it from deceiving Eve. But also remember that the Lamb of God had been slain from the foundation of the world." D stopped as if he, too, was fascinated by what was being said. He looked at the others, and he saw that their jaws had dropped because of such a revelation.

"It was God's eternal plan to birth sons and daughters after His own image, and for that to happen, He had to use Himself—Jesus, the Word of God! The Father became flesh so that all who would accept the sacrifice of Christ would die to the desires of the flesh and become like Him." D stopped. He appeared to fight what the Spirit wanted him to say. The others looked at one another with surprise. They had never seen D fight the anointing as he was then.

"Let the Spirit speak, D," Brenda boldly commanded.

"I … I do not want to," D admitted, trembling. "All that He has taught me and I've experienced …" D trailed off as tears begin to stream from his eyes.

"D, what's wrong?" asked Marcus.

"Yeah, what's the matter?" Bobby asked, concerned.

D begin to cry loudly as he also started repenting for not being a vessel worthy of the Lord. The others could feel D's pain, for they, too, felt insufficient. But it would be the Lord Himself, Jesus, who appeared to comfort them. "Why are you afraid?" the Lord said. "You are no longer just flesh and blood but born of My blood shed for each of you. What I am, so are you. If I am of My Father, then so are you, for I and My Father are one."

The room turned into praises and thanksgiving with the presence of the Lord. The group fell to their knees and lowered their heads to the floor to give complete homage to their King. But He was much more than just their King. He was their big brother! No one knew how long they praised the Lord, and for that matter, no one cared! Most had seen the essence of the Holy Spirit and had felt the anointing surging through their being, but this was the first time they had seen Jesus! Their hearts burned with such great compassion that they could not contain themselves as their shouts of joy rang out. What if someone heard them? What if someone called the police? It did not matter, for they were lost in the worship of their Lord!

When Jesus left and they all were eased from the anointing and their thoughts were made clear, they could only look at one another. What had just happened was very real and was still vivid in their minds. There was no longer any doubt about just who and what they were. They knew that the war that they had been training for was to be fought in the spirit realm and that it would affect what would happen in the physical world. They were to use the many things that the Spirit had taught and shown them there and eventually in the physical world. They were the sons and daughters of the Most High!

Everyone now understood why the Spirit had given them the dreams. They were to affect change, and they now knew how. At that moment the Spirit spoke to D and told everyone to stand. They all could feel the presence of the Father. It was a marvelous feeling, but this time there was a strangeness about it. D told everyone to hold hands. When they were all holding hands, they were translocated to the spirit realm.

They all recognized the place where they were. They could hear the sounds of gunfire. People were screaming, "Help me. Save me." Some people were running around, seeking cover from those who were shooting. The group saw some black gangbangers shooting at some whites who were also armed with guns. They threw the occasional bomb between them, and there were bursts of automatic gunfire intermittently. The Spirit had placed the group in a war zone! However, no one felt threatened or afraid. They could feel the protective aura from the Spirit surrounding them. They realized that they had entered into the war that was to come.

The Spirit seemed to speak to all of them at once. "What you see is the result of man allowing the wiles of the enemy to overcome them. The white racists thought that they could easily destroy the people of color. What they failed to understand was that many blacks and Latinos had been trained in urban warfare way before this time."

The group fully understood, especially Bobby, Miguel, and Marcus, all of whom were ex-gangbangers. As they looked out at the gory scene, most of them became teared up, for they knew that many of those people were going to die that day. Of that they had no doubt! Why had America—and the rest of the world—allowed this? Surely, some leaders had warned others about such a time! Yet those voices had not been loud enough.

"Blacks, whites, Latinos, and all races will be involved," continued the Spirit. "Political leaders thought that the terrorists were the threat, but they did not see the trick from the enemy. America will be decimated, and many will be lost. Even so, this is not Armageddon but a chance for many to be saved." There was silence. Brenda could hear the others weeping. She could feel her own tears streaming down her face. She wanted to wipe her eyes, but she feared that if she stopped holding the others' hands, the protective aura would be broken. "You all must go forth and save those who have the mark of Christ upon their souls.

Be it black, white, or whoever, the work of the Lord is now upon you. Remember your training. Do not falter with the spiritual gifts He has bestowed upon you. And most of all, fear not the enemy, for I am with you always." With that, they each relaxed and released their hands. They looked at one another, and knowing what each of them had to do, they went forth, each in different directions.

And so it begins!

Printed in the United States
By Bookmasters